Place In This World

J. Adams

J. Adams

Library of Congress Control Number: 2011906224

Cover design by Laura J Miller
anaurthorsart.com

The proverbial light at the end of the tunnel, or the pot of gold at the end of the rainbow, is nothing more than fate's delivery of one to his rightful place; a place that is predestined, yet will only be acquired after conquering the raging storm that is the world.

J.A.

Shelter

Rubbing her lightly covered arms against the frigid cold, Elina trudged through deep drifts of snow, knowing that if she stopped, she would surely freeze to death. She probably would anyway.

Before escaping her captor she had managed to trade her tattered robe for a cotton tunic, leather leggings, and boots that were two sizes two big and had seen better days. The thin shawl she tightened around her shoulders did nothing to warm her against the fierce winds that blew against her face, burning the cut on her chapped lips and the open wound on her forehead. By rights she shouldn't have felt any pain in the numbing air. She shouldn't have felt anything after hours of exposure.

She kept her head down and continued to walk, her frail body battling against the elements that assaulted her. She was surrounded by desolation as far as the eye could see. There was absolutely nowhere to seek shelter or refuge. No mountain crevices, no trees, no bushes, nothing to even lend the illusion of shelter. The land was flat and void of any life but hers, and the only thing that disturbed the desolate landscape was the sound and sight of a single set of footprints crunching in the thick blanket of snow. Hers. It was one of the bleakest sounds she had ever heard, coming second only to the sound of her captor's footsteps approaching the door of the tower room she had been locked in for the past year.

She escaped and she was free now. But to what end? She didn't know where she was going or what she was going to do, only that she must keep moving. The evil and vile powers that be would not simply let her go. She knew she would be hunted–hunted until she was found, then made to pay for the trouble of having to be captured. And even if she was not found, she was sure she would forever see her captor's face when she slept.

So she would never sleep, at least not for a very long time.

The mass of long, dark, spiraled ringlets she'd hastily braided had now come loose and she futilely tried to keep it out of her face. Not that the view was even worth looking at. Besides, her eyesight was slowly beginning to blur with each exertion-filled step. Each step found her weakening
and her strength waning. A couple of tears fell from her eyes and froze on her cheeks.

I must keep going. Must not . . . stop.

Even as she mentally repeated the commands, she knew she would not make it. At that moment she realized she couldn't take another step. She tried, but she couldn't move. The desolate world around her began to spin and she felt herself falling, with one last coherent thought filtering through the eerie silence of her mind.

My life is at an end . . . and I shall never see the sun again.

She was completely oblivious to the sound of the

winged being that gracefully landed next to her in the snow, or the strong arms that enfolded her before taking flight once again.

One

Rescued

A fire crackled in a small pit in the cavern hidden in the side of a mountain. Light and heat permeated the surroundings and the popping sound of burning wood echoed against the chamber walls. Awaking to a feeling of warmth, Elina grimaced as she turned to her side on the soft fur-covered pallet made of pine boughs. She tried to clear her throat, grimacing again at the pain the effort wrought. She struggled to open her eyes but couldn't because the light burned them and the pain was excruciating.

Where am I? was her first half coherent thought. *I*

have to keep going.

Just as she began to moan and struggle a bit, she felt a gentle hand begin stroking her hair and a deep voice softly crooning in a mixture of English and a language she had never heard before.

"You are safe, *sashana. Etalamai, sashana.* Be at peace. *Talimaich etn.* I will take care of you."

The comforting voice and touch calmed her, eased her discomfort, and slowly lulled her back to sleep.

Nilan continued to croon softly, more now in his native tongue than English. When the young woman's breathing became deep and even once more, he sighed and tucked the fur blanket snugly around her. He sat unmoving and watched her sleep. She was a strong one, this young human woman he had now taken it upon himself to protect. He knew neither her name nor her past, yet he knew *her.*

It was obvious that the woman was running from a dangerous situation. The danger clearly showed on her face He had tended to her injuries after getting her warm. Beneath the bruises, Nilan saw the beauty she possessed. He had momentarily glimpsed the violet color of her eyes and saw the vulnerability in them. She had a look of frailty, but he knew that would change once she had regained her strength. Other than the bruises, she bore none of the marks of other humans. She was unbranded. He stared at her for a moment longer.

How could a human stay so pure in a place riddled with so much darkness and unrest?

Pondering that thought, he finally stood, walked over to the fire, and stretched out his massive wings so they could fully dry. This was something he would have normally done first thing, but there were other things that were more important than his comfort. Now that he was sure the young woman was on the mend he could tend to his own needs.

Closing his eyes, Nilan stood before the fire and pondered the evil that had grown and spread over this part of the world since his arrival over five hundred years ago. Instead of traveling with the rest of his people to Krisandor, he had chosen to come here, to the kingdom of Dominae and help wherever he could. He had known that he would miss his people dearly, but he had felt certain that coming to Dominae was right. Saying goodbye to his family was hard. He clearly remembered the day he parted from them.

"Will you not reconsider and come with us? his sister asked.

He shook his head and looked into her eyes. "Please understand, I must do this."

She heaved a resigned sigh. "I do understand."

"I cannot explain it, but a part of me is driven to do this. I know not what calls me, only that I must heed that calling."

His sister touched his cheek. "You must follow the promptings of your heart. Just know that
King Cillian will always welcome you into Krisandor. You have a home there."

Pulling himself to the present, Nilan pondered the strong surety he had felt then. Now as he flew to and fro observing this crumbling part of the country, he was no longer certain. He wasn't certain about anything anymore. With evil abounding in every form imaginable, he'd finally made the decision to leave and

join the rest of the Inchant people in Krisandor. Then he
happened upon

the human woman in the snow–and his heart, a heart
that had never been touched, a heart that was

destined to be closed forever to the most powerful of
emotions, was wrenched open with a force that

could not be ignored.

She was all alone. And so was he.

She was not of his kind.

He was not of her world.

He had been set to leave this vile kingdom.

To leave it and its inhabitants to their fate.

That was before he saw her.

Hearing a slight movement, Nilan opened his
eyes and froze. The young woman was awake and
staring at him.

When Elina finally forced her eyes open, the last
thing she expected to see was the splendid being before
her. Even in her weakened state she was full of awe.
Never had she ever seen anything so beautiful. She'd

heard people speak of Inchants, but she always dismissed the talk as the imaginings of man. And now here she was, lying before one.

His shoulder-length straight hair was the color of spun gold and seemed to blend in with his skin. His eyes were a clear hazel and his masculine features were absolutely astounding. The white tunic hung open on his tall, muscular frame, with slits cut in the back giving his golden wings freedom from obstruction. He was the most perfect thing she had ever seen in her life. She continued to stare at him, wide-eyed.

Nilan slowly lowered his wings and tied up his tunic.

"Do not be afraid," he softly said in a sing-song voice.

"I am not afraid," Elina rasped, her voice hoarse from exposure to the elements.

She watched him slowly approach her. When he reached her side, he knelt by the pallet and pressed a gentle hand to her forehead. She relaxed and absorbed the warmth of his hand.

"The fever has broken," he said, looking into her eyes. "How do you feel?"

"Thirsty."

He quickly stood and ladled some water into a carved wooden cup. He had gone back out earlier and gathered some snow and melted it to clean her injuries and brought extra to drink. He knelt again and held her head up a bit, holding the cup to her lips.

Elina took a sip of the water and swallowed painfully. She took a few more sips before declaring she'd had enough. She looked up into Nilan's eyes as he gently lowered her head.

"Thank you," she said softly.

"You are welcome." He placed the cup on the ground. "Are you warm enough?"

"Yes, thank you. Not only for this, but for saving me from certain death . . . It was more than kind of you."

"I help when and where I can," he said as if it were nothing.

But it was something to her. She would never be able to express her gratitude that he had come when he did. "I have heard stories about your people, and even about you. I thought they were just that, myths and stories."

Nilan smiled sadly. "I suppose you would. I am sure many others feel the same."

Elina felt drained again and she knew she needed to rest while she could, but she also wanted to know more about her rescuer.

"Do you have family?" she asked.

"Yes," he answered. "But they live in another kingdom."

"How sad for you . . . to be alone."

He did not comment. "What is your name?" he asked instead.

"Elina. And yours?"

"Nilan."

"I am pleased to meet you, Nilan."

He smiled. "I am pleased to meet you as well, Elina, though I wish it were under better circumstances." He looked at her intently. "Tell me, Elina, from whom were you running?"

"From . . . someone very dangerous," she answered, closing her eyes against the burning tears that immediately began to seep through. "I cannot let him find me," she whispered.

He placed a calming hand over hers. "What is his

name?"

Elina hesitated. She hated even saying the name, and just the thought of him nauseated her.

"His name is Thenoch."

Nilan's eyes darkened upon hearing the name, for he knew this man.

Thenoch was one of the most evil people to have ever lived. Once a member of the brotherhood of dark lords, Thenoch escaped from Ubal's kingdom over half a millennium ago when Ubal began killing off the lords, and had lived in exile. Others followed him across the desolation known as The Vast Lands. Unbeknown to Ubal, Thenoch eventually created his own kingdom. After the war between Ubal's people and the Krisandorians, the few people remaining alive who hadn't participated in the war, left Jubilus in search of Dominae and swore their allegiance to Thenoch. He was vile, ruthless, and conniving. He was without morals and without principals, and he thrived on the suffering of others. His every waking moment was spent bringing misery upon everyone he could. Everything he touched was ruined by his wickedness. It was said that he had no soul. Most people tended to agree, but that did not stop them from following him. It seemed Thenoch took over where Ubal left off. In the ten years since the war, the people of Dominae had managed to surpass Jubilus in both weakness and wickedness. Men lied, cheated, and took from his neighbor that which was not his. If one man was offended by another, the offended man would report the other, thus dooming him to deal with Thenoch's wrath. The kingdom was full of greed, vanity, jealousy, immorality, and all that was wicked, yet these things were made to seem good. It was a very lost land of people.

Nilan shifted his thoughts. "I assume Thenoch is angry because you have resisted his evil and his attempts to force his will upon you."

Wiping her eyes, Elina said, "You assume correctly. I would not bow down and swear my loyalty to him, no matter how much he tried to beat me into submission."

"How did you escape?"

"Thenoch made the mistake of hiring a goon who actually had a conscience. After he beat me again, the man helped me to escape. Sadly, he has probably paid for that choice dearly by now." She paused, swallowing hard against the emotion in her throat. "But I know not where to go to find safety."

Nilan looked at her for a moment in silent contemplation before speaking again. "My home is in the forest on the other side of Dominae's Dark Valley. You would be safe there."

Elina looked at him through tear-filled eyes, not knowing what to say. She wanted to accept his help, but she was afraid of putting him in danger. She had been alone in the world for too long. All the joy that once filled her life had been taken away, and until Nilan's rescue, it had been nearly impossible for her to find the good in the world. She hadn't thought there was any good left. Now she saw things a little differently. Still, Nilan was so kind to her, the last thing she wanted was to bring grief upon him.

"Do not fear for me, *sashana*," Nilan said, seeming to read her thoughts. "For I am very capable of protecting myself, and you as well. Besides, in all the years I have lived in Iskin Forest, no one has dared to enter." He smiled ruefully. "I am afraid people are under the impression that the forest is haunted."

A slight smile touched Elina's lips. "And what, I wonder, would give them that impression?"

"I could not venture to guess," he said with a twinkle in his eye.

Elina's smile widened for a moment before she sobered as her mind began to fill with questions. "How will we get there? I do not think I can make the long trip back, and there is also the danger of being seen by one of Thenoch's goons to be considered."

"Elina, how do you think I got here?" There was amusement in his voice.

Realizing the foolishness of her question, her eyes moved to his relaxed wings and she blushed deeply. "I am sorry. I was not thinking."

"Do not apologize. When you have gained more strength, we will leave."

She nodded and closed her eyes, acknowledging that more rest would do her good, wanting to flee to safety as soon as possible. Then again, she did feel safe, even now in this cave out in the middle of nowhere.

"Thank you," she whispered as she drifted back to sleep with that final thought.

Nilan touched a hand to her brow and gently brushed the hair back from her forehead as a feeling of protectiveness he had never felt before swept through him.

"You are welcome, *sashana*," he whispered. He sighed, then stood and moved back to the fire and mentally made his plans.

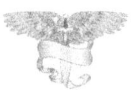

Elina felt cold hands clutching at her in the darkness. The gnarled fingers drew blood as they ripped through the thin fabric of her robe and dug into the tender flesh of her skin. The putrid smell of his breath was thick in her nostrils and throat and she felt herself becoming sick as he taunted her.

"You stupid girl! You can never escape me. You are mine. I own your very soul. It is useless to keep fighting me."

"No!" Elina cried as she struggled to free her arms from the evil one's icy grip. "No! No! No!"

"Shhh. All is well, *sashana*," came Nilan's gentle voice as he placed a calming hand on her forehead. He looked into her wide frightened eyes. "It was only a dream. You are safe."

Elina closed her eyes and took a calming breath, grateful to know she had only been dreaming.

It had all been so vivid and seemed so real, it took several moments for her to stop shuddering. She opened her eyes slightly and took in the familiar surroundings. The flames of the fire cast shadows on the jagged and uneven walls of the cave, the light giving the stones the illusion of dancing shapeless objects. The warmth of the fire seeped into her bones and gave her much needed

comfort. She was safe–safe from Thenoch and his evil minions. And she knew Nilan would protect

her. She would trust him and trust his word. She had no other choice, after all. Surely fate had sent him to her.

After contemplating that thought another moment, Elina closed her eyes and drifted back to sleep to the faint sound of the wind howling outside the cave.

Darkness shrouded the desolate land. A large, black and red meenabird perched itself outside above the cave entrance and craned its long green neck inside. The beady onyx eyes scanned the darkened area, but the creature could not see past the rounded corner that led to the lit cavern. It cocked its bat-like ears and listened to the soft voices for a moment before spreading its massive, deformed wings and taking off toward the city.

Two

Trusting Again

Elina sat wrapped in a fur blanket while Nilan put out the fire and packed a leather bag with the few belongings he'd brought with him. As she watched him, she thought about what he told her about Inchants traveling lightly because they live off the land. Looking at the small bag and the long leather one propped against the cave wall that held his bow, a quiver of arrows, blow gun, and darts, she realized how true the stories she'd heard really were. Not only were Inchants beautiful and ageless but resourceful as well. They were strong and fearless, yet their compassion and courage was unmatched. They truly were a perfect race of people.

The only light that surrounded them now came from a small candle near the wall and daylight coming from the cave entrance. Though the shelter looked different without the fire, it still gave Elina a feeling a safety. Leaving the cave made her both anxious and melancholy at the same time.

Nilan's deep voice softly interrupted her thoughts.

"We should leave now." He pulled the straps of both bags over his arms and swung them round his back.

Elina nodded, dreading leaving the warmth of the cave and having to again face the cold. She stood and pulled the fur tightly around her.

Nilan smiled. "Do not worry, *sashana*. My body heat is considerably higher than that of humans. You will be warm enough."

Elina's cheeks immediately colored. She smiled shyly and looked away. She followed him to the cave entrance, a bout of nervousness quickly coming over her when she contemplated their mode of travel. Having her feet not touching the ground would be new to her and she couldn't help feeling a little afraid.

"Are you ready then?" Not waiting for a reply, Nilan swept her up in his arms.

She blushed deeply as she placed her arms around his neck. Though the warmth radiating from him was comforting, she tensed when he began to extend his wings.

"It is all right," he softly crooned, sensing her fear. "I will not let you fall." He held her eyes with his. "Will you trust me?"

The question was a simple one, yet for Elina, it wasn't. Before being rescued by Nilan, she promised herself that she would never trust anyone again. She had not thought she could. After all, trusting in Dominae was a detriment, and very dangerous to one's health. The slightest lapse of one's guard would seal their fate in seconds, an unbidden fate with no escape. Of course, she had been fortunate. She knew not why her life had been spared or what fate had in store for her, but there had to be a reason the Inchant warrior found her. She could trust him.

Couldn't she?

She sighed. She would not let herself continue on in this mode of thinking. Nilan was not like the others. He was pure and all that was good. Willing her fear away, Elina nodded and forced herself to relax. Nilan continued to hold her gaze with his and before she knew what happened, they were in the air. Elina found herself smiling widely as they gracefully flew over terrain she didn't even realize she had walked. Nestled in Nilan's strong arms she felt warm and safe–safer than she imagined she would feel.

"What do you think?" Nilan asked as his wings pushed them higher.

"This is incredible!" she answered excitedly and he laughed. How she loved his laugh. It was almost musical, the tone of it rich and warm, and she knew she could never tire of hearing it. It was
perfect, just like him.

Reigning in her thoughts, Elina let her eyes sweep the vast snow-covered landscape. It was as desolate as she remembered. How had she walked that far in such weather? She quickly put the question aside. What mattered was she had been rescued, and she was safe now. In the distance she could see the city, the distinct shapes of various buildings coming into view. Thenoch's palace rose above them all, the dark stone spires reaching up like battle-worn lances. She saw the square tower where she had been held prisoner. Sudden panic rose inside her. What if they were seen? Thenoch would come after her for sure and her fate would be sealed.

Sensing Elina's unrest, Nilan tightened his arms around her and said, "Hold on, *sashana*." In the next instant, his powerful wings pushed them up higher until they were hidden in the clouds.

Elina closed her eyes and buried her face against his neck, and wondered how he knew which way to go when she couldn't see two feet in front of her. She consoled herself with the fact that he knew what he was doing. Nilan and his people had been born to conquer the skies. A small gust of cold wind blew against her exposed ear, causing her to shiver a little. She pressed tighter against Nilan and felt comfort in the way he drew her into himself even more. The chill went away as quickly as it came and she wondered anew at the warmth of him.

Feeling a change in altitude after another moment, Elina opened her eyes to see endless acres of green trees beneath them.

"We are here," Nilan said softly before gracefully gliding down into the thick forest.

"How do you know where to land in such a vast forest?" she asked.

He smiled. "It is my home, *sashana*. I know every part of the woods."

She heaved a small sigh of relief, grateful that they had made it to their destination undetected.

Within seconds, Nilan landed in front of a gray stone building that was the size of a cottage. When Elina's feet touched the ground, she briefly let her eyes scan the thick forest surrounding them. Beams of sunlight streamed down through the tall trees and reflected off tiny specks in the gray stone that seemed to shimmer beneath the layer of green moss like precious jewels. There were two large stone columns on either side of the beautifully carved wooden door, and small, white stone figurines of Inchants graced the floral grounds. A cobbled walkway ran from the entrance of the iron fence to the doorway. A picture of a sun, half moon, and three stars was carved in the rectangular white stone placed above the front door with Inchant writing beneath it. Elina studied the writing. It was like none she had ever seen before.

"*Dom ein tikn,*" Nilan said as he watched her trying to read the words. "It means home of peace."

She smiled. "It is beautiful, and the area does look and feel peaceful. How could it not be?" Truly she had never seen a home so lovely. Looking at her surroundings once more, she said, "I don't
know how to thank you for sharing your home with me. And I shudder to think of my eminent demise had you not found me."

"Then think no more on it," he said in a gentle tone. "And there is no need to thank me. For what good are our lives if we cannot help one another?"

Smiling warmly, she replied, "Not much."

Nilan gave Elina a tour his home before taking her to her room. It was not a large home by any
means, but it was all he needed. The castle-like structure bore three sleeping rooms, a garden room next to the kitchen, which was entirely encased in glass, a great room, a formal dining room, and a

bathing room. It wasn't a mansion, but it was beautiful, elegant, and comfortable. He had been happy there and he hoped she would be too.

As Nilan took in the look of wonder on Elina's beautiful face as she studied her surroundings, he thought maybe he could be happy there again. When she turned to him and smiled with that same look, he knew he could. He cleared his throat and changed the course his thoughts.

"I hope you will be comfortable here," Nilan said as he opened the door to the room that would be Elina's.

Elina smiled widely as she entered the most cozy room she had ever seen.

The large iron bed that sat directly in the middle of the room was topped with a thick, white down cover. A white and gold woven rug was placed on the gray marble-tiled floor by the bed. A huge granite chest sat against one wall and a gold framed mirror hung above it. Various paintings of landscapes adorned three walls and a large painting of a beautiful palace hung on the other. A glass figurine of an Inchant mother holding a child sat atop a marble table in a corner. Six potted plants sat on pedestals in various areas of the room, and beneath the bedside table was a stack of books, all leather-bound. There was a fireplace to the right of the bed, and on the mantle sat smaller

glass figurines of Nilan's people.

Elina sighed inward. The room was absolutely beautiful and most inviting. Of the three sleeping rooms, this one was the largest and most elegant. She turned and looked at Nilan, her heart suddenly touched. "This is your room." It wasn't a question.

Nilan smiled. "It is yours now. I will use one of the others."

"I cannot let you do that. This is your home."

"It is your home as well. I want you to be comfortable."

"But one of the other rooms would be just . . ."

"Fine for me," he said, interrupting her. "Please," he insisted.

Elina was warmed by his generosity. "All right," she relented. "Thank you. And not just for the room. I am intruding upon your life, yet you have shown me nothing but kindness. I have no material possessions

28

and nothing to offer you for protecting me, yet you are still willing to do it. Mere words seem trite, but thank you for everything."

Warmed by her words, Nilan softly brushed the back of his fingers against her cheek. "You are most welcome." He dropped his hand and again cleared his throat. "Make yourself comfortable. I must make a short trip to the edge of town." Seeing panic immediately fill Elina's eyes, he took her hand and squeezed it gently. "I will not be away for long, *sashana*. You will be safe. I promise." When she nodded, he gave her a reassuring smile and left.

Three

Aware

"Did you see it, Master?" the short, bald, wrinkled man asked as he approached the figure sitting on a throne in the darkened hall. The only light that existed was the candle the small man held in his leathery hands. The flame illuminated the eyes of the large meenabird perched on a golden stand by the throne. The master's hand repeatedly caressed the bird's feathered back.

"Of course I saw it, you imbecile," he replied with a calm voice.

The man should have known better than to ask

such a foolish question. Of course his master saw it. He saw everything, and until the young woman's escape, he'd never missed anything. Though the man had nothing to do with that particular event himself, he had still been one of the many recipients of the master's wrath. His shoulder still carried the bruise of a wooden club, the result of being unfortunate enough to cross the master's path at the wrong time. He knew better than to speak again unless the master spoke to him, so he stood between the two large stone pillars on either side of the red carpet that stretched to the throne and waited in silence, glancing briefly at the fearsome shadowed figure before lowering his eyes.

If he were to lose his eyesight tomorrow, he would never forget that haggard, hideous face. It was imprinted in his mind every waking moment. It haunted his dreams at night. Every deep line. Every huge pockmark. Every oozing open sore on his forehead. Even the ones that oozed beneath the scraggly strands of hair on his dome-shaped head. No, each and ever feature of the master was branded in his mind. The creature that in no way resembled a human anymore had seen to it.

"Are you not going to ask me what I intend to do?" the master asked, pressing his gnarled hands together, his index fingers straightening to make a steeple beneath his chin. "Are you not curious about what action I intend to take?"

Knowing he needed to choose his words carefully, the man hesitated only for a moment. Daring to raise his eyes, he answered, "I need not ask, Master Thenoch, for I know you are wise and have no need to satisfy the curiosity of one so lowly as myself."

A gravelly rumble resonated from Thenoch's chest. "How true. However, I will answer the question that you are too spineless to ask." He paused and smiled.

The little man knew that smile. He had seen it hundreds of times, and it definitely wasn't the kind of smile that warmed the cockles of one's heart. No, it was quite the opposite. It wrought fear in those who were unfortunate enough to be recipients of it.

"What will you do?" he finally asked, figuring he had nothing to lose at this point.

Thenoch laughed. "Located a little backbone, have you? Well, if you really must know, I intend to do . . . absolutely nothing." He smiled at the startled expression on his pitiful excuse for a servant's face. "There is no need for me to do anything right now. The time will come soon enough for me to show everyone that Inchants are not as immortal as we have been led to believe." His eyes narrowed. "No one takes what is mine. And before the blood-red sun has risen seven more times, I will not only have my property back, but Nilan's heart on a platter as well."

Kill an Inchant? Impossible! The man silently reasoned.

"You think it impossible?" Thenoch asked, apparently reading his thoughts. "Well, Lucius, my unbelieving servant, I tell you it is not. And soon I will prove it." He stood and stared down at the frightened man who immediately bowed his head. "The life of that winged man will soon be prematurely terminated."

Four

A Storm Brewing

Nilan continued to scan his surroundings as he stood in a small shop on the edge of town. The wind howled outside, adding a bite to the chilling cold. Only a few small buildings stood here and there–there was snow on the ground and the roads were icy. Before leaving the forest, he had checked the area to make sure no one was out.

He watched the short blind woman as she wrapped several robes, a brush, comb, mirror, and other accessories he'd picked out for Elina in a piece of beige material and tie it securely with a rope.

Her back was curved, her fingers gnarled, but somehow she deftly formed a bow with the rope. Lifting her milky gray eyes, she smiled and handed him the bundle.

Until now Nilan had never frequented any of the shops. He'd never had reason to because the forest supplied him with everything he needed, and since the changing of the land had begun, he usually kept close to his home. The evil that now filled the hearts of the people made it pointless for him to offer his help. No one needed it. They now had their god. Thenoch.

Still, Nilan knew this woman to be kind. At least she was once. He sensed a change in her and it saddened him. When she had inquired about his purchases, he told her they were presents for a friend. He would not disclose Elina's identity or her presence. He reminded himself that he could trust no one. Keeping conversation to a minimum, he paid the woman, thanked her and left.

Krisandor

King Cillian sat on a granite bench in the palace courtyard, a wide smile lighting his face as he watched his daughter and son-in-law play with their nine-year-old son and seven year old daughter.

He loved his daughter with all his heart and couldn't have wished for a better husband for her, and he completely adored his grandchildren. His heart was filled with gratitude that Ciran and Isiral had successfully completed their journey in Jubilus and had come back to him.

The war between the two kingdoms had been brutal and emotionally painful for Cillian, for he had lost so many he loved, people who had been swayed by Ubal's treachery during the course of their journey to the point that they gave up their chance to re-enter Krisandor and return to their loved ones. His heart still ached for the ones who had fallen. But alas, he knew there was nothing he could have done. They all had their agency. They each made their choice. They chose a life of evil over a life of love. As a result, they lost everything.

Because of the valiant and pure hearts of the

Krisandorians, their bodies had since undergone a change and they were becoming immortal. So were their surroundings. The kingdom had always been beautiful, but now it was even more so. Colors, smells, sights, and sounds were more vivid. The laughter that had always rung in the air was more musical. It was all beyond description, and this new beauty would never fade.

Cillian thought with sadness of all the ones who missed their chance of receiving this great gift, as well as the ones who would miss it still. Then he closed his eyes and put the memories where they should be–in the past, and concentrated on the pressing matter before him. He felt, more than heard his son approach. He turned and smiled as Sakriel sat next to him on the bench, his son's features mirroring his own so perfectly. He reached for his son's hand and squeezed it firmly.

"It seems your gift is yet needed, son. Can you feel it?"

Sakriel nodded. "Yes, father. It is faint, but it is there."

"There are only a few, but those few are important. There are two others in particular who will need our aid."

Sakriel looked into his father's eyes. "What is your will, father? I will do anything you ask of me."

Cillian placed his arm about his son's shoulders, his insides swelling with pride. "For now, we must prepare for the pending storm."

Thenoch stood in a secret room below his sleeping chamber. The room was extremely cold, and puffs of fog escaped him with each breath. He drained a goblet of thick red liquid and knelt on the hard earth before the stone pool of water. Having partaken of an extra potent blend of Splendorfire, he was ready to commune with the dark spirits of the of the underworld. After a moment, the reflection of a scaly face appeared.

"What do you seek?" came the gravelly voice.

"Great Spirit of Darkness, war is near. I wish to know my fate."

The water rippled, distorting the face slightly. "Your fate is uncertain."

"What is meant by this?"

"You fate is uncertain," the voice repeated.

"What is certain?" Thenoch asked, a hint of frustration in his tone.

"Only one will rise victorious, and that victory will be permanent, never to be undone."

"And your counsel?" Thenoch said, bitingly. He didn't like vague answers.

After a moment of silence, the voice said, "Prepare for the victory." Then the face faded. The water rippled and then calmed.

The dark lord smiled.

"Yes, I must prepare. The underworld is on my side. Victory will be mine."

Five

A Fixed Purpose

Nilan hadn't even made it to the door before Elina opened it. He smiled at the relief that filled her eyes and deduced that she must have been watching for his return the entire time. The thought warmed him.

"I told you I would not be long," he said as he handed the to bundle to her.

"What is it?" she asked, staring down at the large package in her hands.

"Clothing and other things you need."

"You did not need to do this."

"I wanted to. Besides," he said, smiling slightly as

he eyed the worn tunic and leggings she wore, "I do not think those clothes can last much longer."

Elina held the package to her chest and Nilan saw the tears of gratitude in her eyes when she raised them to his. When she smiled that beautiful smile, he determined that he would never let her be without anything. He would make sure she was well cared for.

"I will go and put these in the room and help you with the evening meal. I want to make myself useful."

"You are useful. Just having your company is enough."

She smiled and turned to go to her room, then paused. "Thank you again, for everything."

"You are welcome, Elina."

That night, Elina hummed softly as she put her gifts from Nilan away. As she reverently touched the robes, a vision of the last robe her mother made for her came to mind. The pink, purple and red flowers had been hand-stitched with love, and the detail of the designs were both incredible and beautiful. Tears came to her eyes as she remembered the day her mother presented her with the robe after spending countless late nights working on it. Elina had considered the robe her mother's masterpiece. How she wished she had that robe now, if only to have something left of her mother, something that had been touched by her mother's hands.

Sighing, Elina dried her tears. She was grateful for the safety she now felt, but oh, how she missed her family. She knew she always would. She missed her father's loving smile and gentle embraces. She missed her brothers' affectionate teasing and comforting hugs. Her parents and siblings had been her life. Why did they have to die? Why couldn't she have died with them? Without them, her life in many ways felt pointless now.

Elina sat down on the edge of the bed and closed her eyes and thought about her family, the mental pictures of her last moments with them causing tears to burn behind her closed lids. She had been immersed in the memories only for a moment when there came a soft, gentle voice that seemed to speak to her very soul.

"The purpose for your life is fixed, Elina."

Her eyes sprang open. She looked around the room for the owner of the voice but found herself completely alone. Her mind echoed the words the voice carried. *The purpose for your life is fixed, Elina.*

What could it mean?

She suddenly felt guilty for her selfish thoughts. She had everything she needed and there was no point in longing for something that couldn't be changed. She would be grateful for the bounty that was placed before her. After all, her parents had taught her to exercise gratitude in all things. She would do just that.

That evening, Elina stood quietly looking out her window. She watched the sky darken and the stars slowly appear in the heavens. The stars that were once so bright were now lightly veiled and the moon was redder than she had ever seen it. Still, her surroundings were peaceful and she felt safer than she'd felt in a long time. She sighed and smiled slightly, marveling anew at her good fortune. One minute she had been running for her life, the next, she was rescued in a most unfathomable way. Now she had a home again, and heeding her parents' wise council, she truly recognized what fate had given her.

Elina was pulled from her thoughts when a movement outside caught her eye. She leaned forward and peered into the darkness. When her vision adjusted, she quickly recognized Nilan's incredible form. She watched him kneel at the edge of the courtyard amidst the trees, then extend his arms out in front of him and raise his face toward the heavens.

A gentle breeze stirred the leaves in the trees. The same breeze gently blew Nilan's golden locks back from his face. The silky strands shimmered beneath the red of the moon and the effect was mesmerizing. His body was completely still and he held the position so long, Elina wondered how he could remain that way without wavering. She supposed it was a practiced ritual. It had to be. She gathered it must be a form of meditation. She stayed glued to the spot, not able to move or pull her eyes away. She almost felt like she was intruding on something very private, but she couldn't help herself.

Then the magnificent statue moved, startling Elina to her senses. Quickly she moved away from the window and left him to his privacy.

Nilan felt Elina's eyes on him as he meditated, but it hadn't bothered him in the slightest. Her gaze had actually been quite calming. He wasn't sure why that was. He only knew he had felt a strong stirring of peace. He stood and turned, his eyes resting on the now shaded window, and immediately pondered what the coming days would bring. There would be changes in his life. There already were. Elina's presence had changed everything. He found that life had great meaning again, and his had a new purpose. Now his main priority would be keeping her safe, a priority he felt both compelled and honored to fulfill.

Six

Light Amid Shadow

Elina's morning had been occupied with reading and pondering. She tried to busy herself around her new home with cleaning and straightening, but there really wasn't much to do in that respect. The place was immaculate. She wondered if there was ever a time it wasn't. Of course, before she came, Nilan had lived alone and the home was never graced with company, so it basically remained clean. So for now, her time was her own.

She thoroughly enjoyed reading the book she picked from under Nilan's bedside table. It was a literary work by an author she was quite familiar with who once lived in the kingdom of Anglann. He died over a thousand years ago, but his works were timeless and always would be. He wrote of achieving freedom from the bondage and restraints of evil in life, and there were many. He also wrote of the grandeur of the mind, heart, and spirit that came as a result of choosing that freedom.

Elina loved this book. Her own copy, given to her by her parents, was destroyed along with her home and most of her other personal belongings. She was grateful to be able to read the author's inspiring words again, for now she understood more clearly the meaning of those words. She continued to ponder them through the rest of the day. They gave her peace.

In the city, the feeling in the air was the opposite of peace. Due to Thenoch's order, the time of the daily sunrise meeting had been changed and was now being held at sunset. Once again, the members of the town gathered in the "worship room" of Thenoch's castle.

The room was massive and circular, and porcelain statues of Thenoch lined the walls all the way around. The windows were set high and the ceiling was one giant glass dome, allowing the fading sun of late afternoon, and the red moon at night, to shine down on the worshipers.

There, beneath the dome, they all stood and began the ritual they had begun practicing centuries before. Hands were held high, eyes were closed, and bodies swayed as they chanted over and over again the words they were taught. The words had become a part of them now, and their souls were no longer their own.

Except for a scattered few.

These individuals only pretended to worship, not letting the words pierce their hearts. Disobedience was punishable by death, therefore every part of them obeyed Thenoch's laws. Every

part, that is, except their hearts. Still, the small few conformed and swayed and chanted the words that literally embittered the soul.

Thenoch is god. We are his.

Thenoch is darkness, therefore we worship the darkness.

In darkness, there is life. In Thenoch, there is life.

As the voices rose and swelled, the swaying increased, slowly reaching frantic proportions. Outside the wind howled against the windows. It was as if the frenzy inside called to the very elements of nature, and nature could not resist the beckoning.

Then Thenoch's gravelly voice filled the room and all chanting and swaying ceased.

"My children, my brothers and sisters. Once again your place in my kingdom is assured."

Nothing else was said. There never was. The guards then opened the doors and the people were dismissed.

Seven

Shared Hearts

The afternoon sun was beginning to fade, but Elina still felt its lingering warmth through the shady trees. She found her surroundings peaceful, and safe. She sighed contentedly as she silently worked with Nilan, picking vegetables in the small garden behind his home to have for dinner. The soreness from two days before was gone and her energy level had returned to normal. The bruises on her face were starting to fade. She was beginning to feel like herself again, only better. It was a relief to not have the constant worry of being found hanging over her.

They filled the straw basket with carrots, celery, and broccoli. Elina then followed Nilan over to a small wood and wire fence where they picked a couple of bunches of dark grapes. They looked delicious, just like everything else. She watched Nilan pull one from the bunch.

"Try one," he said, holding it in front of her mouth.

The action took her by surprise. Shyly, she leaned forward and opened her mouth. A feeling of warmth encompassed her as his finger lingered on her bottom lip. A blush quickly heated her cheeks.

"It is wonderful," she said, gazing into his eyes before quickly looking away.

He smiled. "The seeds are from Iriedora, my homeland. They produce abundantly all year long." He stared into her eyes quietly for a moment. "I think we have enough," he said, finally pulling his gaze away and looking at the full basket.

Elina nodded, still composing herself. Her eyes traveled around the plentiful garden. "How is it that it is so warm here in the forest when it is freezing everywhere else?"

Nilan quietly gazed around his fruitful surroundings for a moment. He gestured to a small granite bench and they sat down. He placed the basket on the ground, pushed a strong hand back through the golden tendrils that had escaped his ponytail and sighed.

"It is the wickedness of man that creates the treacherous weather in Dominae." He paused, again casting his eyes around the forest surrounding them. "The forest is spared because no human dares to enter. However, like Iriedora, I am sure it is only a matter of time before it will be affected."

"Iriedora must have been beautiful."

"It was," Nilan said, wistfully. "The soil was very fertile for planting food. The wildflower colors were so vivid and the scent so sweet that the senses could not retain it all. The wildlife was plentiful and my people lived in harmony with every living creature in the forest. Even the trees themselves communed with us."

"The trees?" Elina questioned, a look of fascination filling her eyes.

"Yes," He answered with a smile. "When I was a child I used to sit beneath one tree in particular. The trunk was ten feet wide and the branches curled around one another. There were

small holes at the base of the trunk where some squirrels made a home for themselves. I would sit

for hours studying each and every inch of that tree until I knew it. It knew me as well and we fed a

natural energy to one another. It sensed my presence and made me aware of it."

"That is amazing," Elina said in awe.

Nilan nodded. "All of the trees were ancient, and oh, what stories they could probably tell. The word beautiful did not do Iriedora justice."

"It sounds wonderful," Elina said with a sigh.

"It was." He paused, looking up through the trees. "Iskin will also remain beautiful, until a Dominae citizen enters. Any unclean thing that comes into the forest will drive all that is good away."

"What about me," Elina asked with a teasing smile."I am a citizen of Dominae."

Nilan looked into her eyes intently. "There is only goodness in you. If your heart was not pure,

the land on which you stand would know." His eyes grew soft, as did the musical richness of his voice.

"And so would I."

"Thank you," she said softly.

"I only speak the truth, *sashana*."

She smiled at him, her curiosity suddenly getting the best of her. "Nilan, what does *sashana* mean?" She had wondered about the word ever since the first time he had used it. She thought it must be something the Inchant men called their women.

Nilan didn't answer right away. She continued to look at him expectantly, wondering why he hesitated. Suddenly afraid that her prying had offended him, she said, "I am sorry. It is not my place to ask such things." The last thing she wanted to do was offend him, not after he'd shown her so much kindness and given so much of himself.

"There is no need to apologize," Nilan said, staring into her eyes. The question caught him off guard and he had not been prepared, nor had he been prepared for the emotions the answer wrought.

He wanted to tell her everything that was in his heart, wanted to share the feelings that had awakened in him the moment he first saw her face. But he was afraid–afraid of frightening her.

After all, he was an Inchant warrior.

And though her heart was pure, she was still a human.

They were from two different worlds.

Suddenly, he felt a desperate need to read her thoughts. To know what she was feeling, and what was going through her mind at that moment. But alas, he couldn't let himself intrude in her mind that way. Her personal thoughts were hers and hers alone. Maybe sometime in the future he

would earn the privilege of connecting with her in that way.

Maybe. If he was fortunate.

When she continued to look at him expectantly, he decided to tell her the meaning. Inchants

were an honest people. He would not be anything less.

"*Sashana* means 'my beautiful one.'"

Elina continued to stare at him. Then she touched the fading bruises on her face as her eyes filled with tears. "But I am not."

Feeling his heart speed up a little, he reached out and took her delicate hands in his large, strong ones.

"Your beauty runs deep, *sashana*. The bruises on your face will eventually fade completely . . . and I hope to be able to heal the bruises on your heart as well."

At once, Nilan saw emotion flood Elina's countenance. He felt it, just as surely as he felt her hands in his.

She turned her face away from him as tears began to fill her eyes. His hand tightened around hers. Closing her eyes, she whispered, "You already have."

Nilan closed the space between them. He gently turned her face back to him and took her in his arms. He closed his eyes and pressed a kiss into her hair, inhaling the sweet scent of it. He felt her breath on his neck as she pressed her face into the curve of it and he melted against her warmth. Having her in his arms was the most perfect feeling he had ever experienced. Nothing else mattered. Not her past or where she came from, nor the circumstances that led them to each other. All that mattered or existed was this moment.

Moving back slightly, he tilted her face with his fingers and kissed her.

With that kiss, the life he once knew was no more.

With that kiss, his life was forever changed.

Elina was spellbound by Nilan's kiss, and the scent of him was intoxicating. She wondered how she could deserve such bliss. How had she garnered the affections of this beautiful and astoundingly perfect being? What had she done to warrant such a glorious blessing? She felt his emotions, and the feelings they wrought inside her own heart were beyond description. She wrapped her arms around his neck and pressed one hand into his golden hair while the other pressed down against the smooth feathers of his wings. Her mind kept arguing that this couldn't be happening, but her heart was without doubt.

Nilan broke the kiss and drew back slightly to look into her eyes. "Bind yourself to me, *sashana*. You are a part of me now, just as I am a part of you. I can bind us. All Inchant men are given the power to perform the sacred ceremony when we are young." He kissed her once more and whispered, "Be my wife, Elina."

Momentarily struck speechless by Nilan's passionate request, Elina finally found her voice and said, "But I am not of your people." She rested a hand against his chest and felt his heartbeat keeping in time with her own. "How can we?"

Nilan smiled and buried a hand in her spiraled tresses, in awe of the strength of his feelings. Her statement had been a concern to him as well, for the body chemistry of an Inchant was completely different from that of a human. While a human could live thousands of years before their

bodies began to feel the change of mortality, Inchants underwent no such change, and unless an Inchant's life was interrupted by murder, they lived forever. There had never been a binding between

and Inchant and a human before. They would be the first.

"It does not matter," he finally said. "Our love will be enough." Allowing his mind to finally enter hers, he said through thought, *Yes, sashana, I do love you. I have from the moment I found you in the snow.*

Elina smiled as a tear rolled down her cheek. "I know there is no need to tell you my feelings, for I can feel you in my thoughts, but I will voice them just the same." She pressed a hand to his face and caressed it softly. "I love you. You became the owner of my heart the moment I awakened in the cave and saw you standing before the fire."

He smiled, pressed his forehead against hers, and closed his eyes a moment, soaking in the warmth of her affections. "Will you bind yourself to me?" he asked opening his eyes. "Will you be mine forever, until the end of time?"

Elina nodded, happiness filling her entire being. "I will be yours even longer than that." She leaned forward and kissed him."

They held each other another moment, reveling in their love. Sighing, Nilan finally released her and stood. He picked up the basket and held a hand out to Elina, never moving his eyes from hers. She took his hand and they went into the house to prepare dinner, even though neither of them were hungry now.

Beneath the dark lord's sleeping chamber, the

water in Thenoch's prophecy pool began to bubble and hiss. The whispers of the inhabitants of the underworld echoed off the stone walls and raised to angry groans and wails of excruciating agony. Steam rose from the pool as great drops of water splashed on the ground, each turning to blood the moment it touched down. The bloody drops then changed from red to gray, freezing where they fell, and the voices hissed a single word that rang throughout the room and lingered in the silence long after the bubbling stopped.

"Eeeliinaaa!"

Eight

Soul To Soul

Elina and Nilan washed the vegetables in a large porcelain bowl and cut them up before arranging them on a silver dish. She watched him slice some of the roasted pheasant he had caught
a few days before he left his home. He'd caught some fish as well and had left them in a cooling chamber built in the kitchen wall. Never being one to waste food and only killing what he intended
to eat, Nilan was grateful the meat would be put to use after all.

"Tell me of your life," he said as he placed slices

of meat on a thin wooden tray. "Tell me of your family."

Elina paused in her work as she pondered the events of her life. "I was born in Anglann a hundred and one years ago last week. Which reminds me," she suddenly paused. "How old are you?"

"In your years I am nine hundred and five." He smiled at Elina's surprised expression. "Among my people, full maturity is reached at five hundred years old. After that, the numbers really do not matter."

Elina took a moment to let that sink in. She grinned. "You do not look a day over two hundred."

Nilan laughed softly. "Thank you, *sashana*. Now, back to your life."

"Oh yes," she continued. "I was raised with two older brothers." She smiled as she thought on her family. "My parents were very loving and kind. And I still miss them." She put the knife down. "Two years ago, several of Thenoch's men broke into our home and demanded that my family pledge ourselves to Thenoch. My brothers and I had been away, but when we approached our home and saw the dangerous looking men, my brothers took me to our safe shelter, built a mile away from our home beneath the earth. It was stocked with enough food and water for at least six months."

She closed her eyes and sighed painfully, then opened them and looked at Nilan through the tears. "They never came back for me. After a few days, I left the shelter and went to my home. Most of it had been destroyed. I found my parents and my brothers there, all of them dead, and their bodies in various parts of our home."

Nilan placed the tray of meat on the small kitchen table and went to her. She relished the feel of his arms around her and soaked in the comfort he gave. He pressed his lips against her forehead and continued to hold her close.

"How did you stay free for so long?" he asked, caressing her hair.

She sighed against his shoulder. "I took everything I could carry that was not destroyed back to the shelter and stayed until the food and water ran out. I marked each day that passed. When I finally emerged from the shelter, a year had passed. I thought I would be all right and that Thenoch had probably forgotten about me. I was wrong. I made the mistake of trusting people I thought were friends of my family. Soon after, someone turned me in. I knew then that I could trust no one." She pulled back a little and smiled into his eyes. "And I never have, until you."

Nilan could feel the pain that still ran deep inside her. He wanted to take the pain away, to insure her that he would never let anyone hurt her again. He held her eyes with his. *You are safe now, my beloved. No harm will ever come to you again. I will give my life to protect you. Let your mind be at peace.*

Elina smiled and touched his face, freshly amazed at the way he communicated his feelings to her. *I love you*, her mind spoke to his, and she smiled when he silently returned her feelings.

"Come," he said, taking her hand in his. "Let us eat."

She squeezed his hand and nodded, putting all unhappiness from her mind.

"He was here," the blind woman told Lucius as

he placed two gold coins in her hand, double the going rate for information of importance.

"You are certain?" he pressed, anxious to give his master the information.

"Quite certain," the woman said, slightly miffed. "I know his scent. He assisted me out in the growing fields years ago. It's not the kind of scent you forget." The familiar fragrance of pine and wildflowers was still fresh in her memory. No one she had ever known smelled like Nilan.

Lucius' eyes were wide in excitement. "And you say he purchased feminine items?"

"Yes, you nitwit! How many times do I have to tell you?" The woman hated repeating herself.

Yes! Yes! Yes!, Lucius silently yelled. "The master will be most pleased," he said, turning and quickly exiting the shop.

That evening, just before dark, Nilan and Elina stood before one another in the small courtyard in front of their home with their hands joined. She wore

a silky white robe that Nilan had purchased
for her and he donned a gold one, the color of which
blended in with his hair and skin. She could see
his heartbeat at the base of his throat and imagined it
beating inside his muscular chest in time with her own
heart.

The courtyard was lit by several candles in
elegant brass holders placed here and there and the
forest was filled with the soft sound of crickets, the low
croaking of frogs, and the soft calling of doves. The
scent of pine circulated through the air, mingling with
the perfume of the flowers in the
courtyard. To Elina, it was a most beautiful and perfect
setting.

Looking into Elina's eyes, Nilan took one of her
small hands, held it against his chest, and in English,
recited the vows of the Inchant binding ceremony.

> **"My blood is your blood,**
> **my heart is your heart.**
> **My body is your body,**
> **and my soul, your soul.**
> **I give myself to you,**
> **I bind my being to yours for all eternity,**

never to be taken away,

and never to part."

Elina smiled at him with eyes full of love and Nilan could not stop the tears that fell down his cheeks, for he loved her more than life itself, and he knew he ever would. Inchants mated forever, and if–when–death separated them, he would never take another mate. He would wait for their souls to be joined again in the life to come.

When Elina took his hand and placed it against her own chest, Nilan felt the racing of her heart, and his answered. He held her gaze with his as she repeated the vows.

"My blood is your blood,

my heart is your heart.

My body is your body,

and my soul, your soul.

I give myself to you,

I bind my being to yours for all eternity,

never to be taken away,

and never to part."

Nilan smiled. He released her hands, lifted the sleeve of his robe, and untied the smaller of two matching leather bracelets. The tan bracelet was trimmed in tiny diamonds and bore the words *Fiyi Nilan*–the wife of Nilan. For centuries he'd worn the bracelet, not knowing if the day would ever come when he would be blessed to give it to another. But the day had come. He was no longer alone. He tied the bracelet around her forearm. Picking up one of the candles, he placed a small flat stone under the bracelet against her skin, and permanently sealed the knot with the flame.

Elina gazed into the eyes of the beautiful being who was now her husband, amazed that she was now bound to someone who had only existed in her dreams–dreams borne of stories she had heard growing up. He was no longer a dream but real. More real than anything she could have ever dreamed. She was in awe of the love they shared, and she knew from this moment on, he would be her life-force, the very essence of her world. She sighed as he took her face between his hands and kissed her, and she knew they truly were a part of each other.

"I have finally found my place in this world," she whispered against his lips.

Pulling back slightly, he said, "Your place has

always been by my side."

They stood intertwined another moment before putting out all the candles and going inside.

Nine

A Coming Change

Krisandor

Dawn was just breaking through the trees of the forest when Mazina awakened with a start. She brushed a hand over her sweat-covered brow, surprised to feel the wetness on her fingertips.

"What is it?" Ansel asked, immediately turning over and raising up.

The Inchant woman hesitated a moment before answering her husband, hoping the feeling that had awakened her would go away, but with each passing second it only became stronger. Mazina looked up into her husband's concerned eyes and opened her mind to his.

I dreamed of darkness, and a land that grows restless. My brother has found happiness, but he is in danger.

Not bothering to question her, Ansel took his wife in his arms and said, "Then we must go and help him." He pressed his cheek against her hair and held her for another moment before rising. "We must speak to Cillian at once."

Elina slowly awakened to a cradle of warmth. She sighed and snuggled deeper in Nilan's embrace. When she felt his lips press softly against her forehead, she opened her eyes and lifted her
face, and found him gazing at her.

"Good morning," she said with a smile and pressed her lips to his.

"Good morning," he murmured, his musical voice low and deep.

Fingering the smooth feathers of his wings, she sighed and pressed her face in the curve of his neck, finding indescribable comfort in his nearness. She wished she could stay this way forever, safe

in the haven of his arms. But she knew that despite the momentary peace she felt, there was still danger lurking beyond the forest. As long as Thenoch was alive there would always be danger.

And what if he discovered she was there? What if Nilan were harmed trying to protect her? What if she lost her husband? Her bond with him was so strong, she couldn't live without him. If she lost him there would be no reason to go on. He was everything to her. And she would die before she let Thenoch take her again. She closed her eyes against the painful thought.

Where had this sudden bout of fear come from?

Nilan felt the shudder that went through Elina. He moved back slightly and placed a hand under her chin, raising her face to his.

"What is it, *sashana?*" When he saw tears begin to fill her eyes, he opened his mind to hers and read her thoughts. He caressed her face softly.

Do not fear, beloved. I will keep you safe. I promise. He dried her tears and kissed her. "I will keep you safe," he whispered. "And all will be well."

72

Elina smiled and kissed him, forcing the fear from her mind. *I trust you, my husband.* She touched his face. *I trust you.*

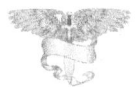

Twelve men knelt before Thenoch's throne. All of them were large and dressed for battle. Each looked straight ahead, never moving their eyes from their leader.

Thenoch looked down at the men, pinning each one with his bloodshot eyes, ready to give them their orders and fully prepared for their response.

"My enemy has acquired a piece of my property." He paused, burning a hole through each man with his eyes. "I want that property back. Tomorrow at dawn, you will enter Iskin Forest and take back what is rightfully mine."

The men suddenly began to murmur amongst themselves. No human had ever dared to enter Iskin Forest because of the rumors of it being haunted. There had been many who reported hearing strange sounds coming from the forest. A few people have even seen dark shapes and moving shadows drifting through the trees. Because of these stories, no one dared to even go near the area.

Now the men were being ordered to enter a section that held an unseen danger, not certain that they would make it back out alive. Thenoch's gravelly voice interrupted the murmur of the men.

"Either you obey my commands or lose your pitiful lives at the hand of The Order." He smiled at the expressions of the men.

No man wanted to face The Order. It was Thenoch's group of elite assassins. The group of thirty men were both vicious and thorough. They delighted in bloodshed and were always eager for the kill. Like Thenoch, they were without morals or feelings. They were inhuman and incapable of fear or remorse. Their very beings were pure evil, just like their leader.

Gin, the leader of the men finally spoke, knowing there was only one choice. Either way, they would die tomorrow.

"We will go."

Of course you will, Thenoch thought as a hideous smile began to spread across his marred face, causing the open sores to ooze pus that ran down the deep crevices. He had a plan, and the lost

lives of the men was just another part of it.

Look at the fear in their faces. Cowards, all of them. Yet they fear me more. Thenoch's smile

widened at this.

"I will reward you for your obedience."

The men stared at him blankly, their thoughts the same.

What good is a reward if you are not alive to receive it?

"I give you leave to go, gentlemen," Thenoch said with a smile, his voice as cold as ice. He watched them exit the throne room. "*Cowards!*"

Ten

Code Of Honor

"All right, men, spread out! Let's do this!"

The men slowly entered the forest. They moved hesitantly through the trees, a few of them jumping at the sounds of the woods. They were afraid of the unseen dangers they imagined lurking

about. However, their fear of Thenoch was greater. His wrath upon their return would be brutal should they emerge from the forest empty-handed.

Gin, the leader of the band of men, along with another man, walked stealthily about a half a

mile in front of the group. His senses were alert to his

surroundings. He had spent the entire night

before building his courage and sharpening his skills. He had also counseled his wife and son on what they would do should he not return. He'd sent them away to safety, but deep down he wondered if where he sent them would even be safe enough to keep them from Thenoch's grasp. Someone would have to pay for the failure of this mission, and Gin was sure Thenoch would exact payment by taking the lives of their families.

Gin wanted no part of Thenoch's plans for Dominae. He never had, but when the lives of his wife and grown son were threatened, he knew he had no choice but to comply to the evil dictator's

wishes. He had thought of traveling with his family the night before, maybe even taking them back

across the Vast Lands to Jubilus, but it was too far. Besides, Thenoch's reach knew no limits and he had eyes everywhere. Just look at what was happening with Elina. Even now, she had no idea of what Thenoch was planning. She probably thought she was safe, that the Inchant would always protect her, yet now they were both in danger. Neither of them had done anything, except manage to be free from Thenoch's vile designs, but he would not leave them in peace. Now Gin and his men were assigned to be their assassins.

Well, for Gin, this day would end badly one way or another. He was sure of it. He thought back on what he'd considered was most likely his last conversation with his wife. She had cried in his arms and he had tried to console her the best he could.

"Come with us," she pleaded as he took them by carriage close to the edge of town in the middle of the night. He had wanted to get his wife and son as far away from Dominae as possible.

"I cannot," he said to her, *"for Thenoch would surely send The Order after me and we would all*
be killed. At least this way, you and Laslow will have some chance of being safe." He took her face in his hands. "Misha, it must be this way."

Gin sighed inwardly and cleared his thoughts, focusing on the here and now. The present was most likely all he had.

Place in This World

Eleven

Moment of Grace

Birds chirped and sang happily as they landed on the bird feeders Nilan made and hung on poles carved from old tree branches. Elina watched them through the kitchen window as they chased one another, stopping to feed before taking off again. She marveled at their freedom and grace, and felt gratitude for these moments that allowed her the opportunity to appreciate the beauty of nature that surrounded them. She almost felt as if she and Nilan were in their own little world, and as she reflected on how different her life was a mere few days before, she felt a renewed awe for the happiness she now had. Nilan's love made up for all the pain she'd suffered and healed her heart, causing the hurts of the past to fade into nothingness.

Elina turned at the sound of the back door opening. Before she could draw a breath, Nilan was standing before her with a bouquet of freshly cut flowers. She smiled widely and took the offered gift, pressing her face in the fragrant bunch and breathing in the floral perfume.

"Thank you," she said, wrapping her arms around his neck and kissing him.

"You are welcome." He held her for a moment.

Nilan had never been so blissfully happy in his life. He had been told by his sister that love was a very intoxicating thing, and with the Inchants it was even more so. He smiled as he remembered Mazina describe her feelings for Ansel.

"You cannot think clearly, because your every thought is consumed with the person who

becomes literally your other half. Your mate becomes the center of your life, and all that matters."

He sighed inwardly, thinking about how true her words were. He missed his sister. He wished he could see her and her family again. Maybe one day.

"I love you, *sashana*," he whispered into her hair.

"I love you."

"Come with me," he said, moving back and taking her hand in his. "There is something I would like you to see. Someplace special I wish to show you."

When they exited the house, Nilan lifted her in his arms, extended his wings and rose above the trees.

"Where are we going?" Elina asked as they flew the opposite direction of town.

"You will see," he said with a smile and glided through the air at a leisurely pace.

The further they went, the more full the forest looked beneath them. It was an endless mass of green and not an empty space to be seen. After another moment, they came to the edge of the forest, and the vision Elina's eyes beheld took her breath away. There was sparkling blue water as far as the eye could see. Nilan landed and set Elina on her feet. She took off her shoes and smiled at the feel of the warm sand between her toes. She stood by her husband's side and silently watched the foamy waves roll inward, washing small seashells ashore. The rays of the setting sun shimmered against the water like gold. She turned to him.

"It is one of the most beautiful things I have ever seen."

Nilan smiled. "This is a very special place for me. I do not think a human has ever set foot on these shores." He smiled ruefully. "Probably because they would have to come through the forest to get here."

"Probably," Elina agreed with a smirk.

He laughed and pulled her close, sobering after a moment. "It has been my place of solitude and
I wanted to share it with you, because solitude is a thing I no longer need." He looked into her eyes and smiled. "You fill every need and longing I have ever had."

Elina pressed a hand against his face as sweet emotion rose inside her. "I feel the same," she said softly before raising her lips to his.

Hearing a strange sound, Elina broke the kiss. "What are those?" she asked, pointing to two large, pink fish-like sea creatures jumping above the waves, then diving back in and repeating the
process.

"Those are Angelin Serpents. They are sea

hunters."

Elina continued to stare at the creatures. Their tails were long and silver, and their bright pink bodies donned wing-like fins. On their heads were long antennae. They were the strangest looking things she had ever seen.

"What do they hunt?" she finally asked.

"Whatever happens to cross their path," Nilan answered. He squeezed her hand, a sly smile tugging at his mouth. "However, they never harm beautiful water nymphs, which is what they would consider you, so you would be safe."

"Is that so?" she said, raising one brow playfully.

He laughed and pulled her close. "Most assuredly."

She turned in his arms, leaned back against his chest and watched the serpents as they continued their play. She laughed as water shot up in the air from a blow hole at the top of one serpent's head.

"Now that is as picture I do not think I will ever forget."

Nilan chuckled behind her ear. "You will not have to. We can come back as often as you like."

"Thank you," she said, reaching back and pressing a hand against his face.

"You are welcome."

She sighed deeply. "There is still some beauty in the world."

"There is indeed, and I shall be grateful for the remaining beauty every day of my life."

"Which will be a very long time," Elina said with a melancholy smile.

"Yes," was all he said.

She turned to face him. "I will be grateful as well." She paused, her thoughts drifting to her parents, her father especially. She thought of how he would have loved to see this part of their world.

"My father used to gaze out over the land and recite something he read from one of the poets of Anglann." She smiled and gave voice to the words.

"The day we can look within ourselves and see our mortality,

yet feel the worth of our souls,

the day we can look on others and see the goodness in them

despite their weaknesses,

the day we can say no to evil,

despite the evildoings of those around us,

when we can cry with those who suffer,

mourn with those who bear loss,

and comfort those who cast your comfort aside,

when we can see the good in each new day

and recognize the gifts that come with that day,

when we can love with a pure heart,

expecting nothing in return,

and magnify our valiance to the fullest,

the day we set aside the cares of the world

and embrace every good thing with a singleness

of mind, heart, body, and soul,

ever faithful, ever vigilant, doing all within

our power to remain unchanged in all respects,

on that day, we become more than mere men—

we become gods

and we live forever."

Elin's final words lingered in the long silence that
followed. Nilan said nothing, but when he smiled she
saw a sheen of tears in his eyes. He turned her to face
the sea again and she relaxed in his embrace. The two
stood and stared over the vast waters, wrapped in their

own world, completely unaware of the evil lurking at the door.

Twelve

Intruders In Iskin

As Nilan lifted Elina in his arms and readied himself for their flight home, his ears tuned in to a distant sound that made his body tense up. It was a sound he'd never before heard in Iskin Forest- the sound of humans ready to make war. He tightened his arms around his wife.

Elina took in the worry now etched in her husband's face. "What is it?" she asked, wrapping her arms around him.

Without answering, Nilan spread his wings and quickly pushed away from the shore. He went higher than normal, wanting to view the danger without being seen.

"What is it?" Elina repeated, her voice giving away her growing fear.

Nilan pressed a calming kiss to her forehead before answering. "There are men in the forest." Taking in her frightened expression, he said, "We will not be seen from up here. I need to see how many there are."

"But what will we do?"

"I will make sure you are safely hidden in the shelter underneath our sleeping room floor. Then I will deal with the danger."

"You knew they would come." It wasn't a question.

"I suspected."

He pressed her protectively against him and she buried her face against his neck as they silently hovered over the group of men. There was no need for Elina to look because they were too high up for her eyes to distinguish any movement in the thick trees. However, Nilan's eyesight was vastly superior to that of humans, during both day and night.

Fixing his gaze down through the deep forest,

Nilan spotted approximately twelve men, all wearing armor and carrying swords and shields. Neither their number or weaponry concerned him.

What did concern him was his wife's safety. He flew back towards their home and slowly descended, landing behind it. He quickly pulled Elina inside and headed to their room.

Nilan took a thick candle from the mantle, lit it and handed it to Elina, then slid their bed over and opened the hidden door.

Elina looked at the set of stairs that led down and then back at Nilan. Tears rose in her eyes. "I am afraid for you."

Nilan pulled her to him, gave her a hard kiss, and hugged her tightly. "I will be all right. Just stay down there and wait for my return. Promise me."

Blinking back the tears, Elina nodded bravely. "I will."

When he released her, she descended the stairs.

Nilan hovered over the opening until Elina reached the bottom. "I promise I will return to you," he said before closing the door.

Elina listened to the sound of Nilan pushing the bed back over the door. Her heart pounded as she thought about the danger he would be in. She forced the thoughts down inside and let her eyes scan the dimly-lit room. It was surprisingly tidy. The floor was laid with flat gray stones. There were two iron chairs and a long stone bench against one wall, and a small wooden table and two chairs against another one. A lantern sat in a corner. There was also a tall wooden cabinet. She walked over and slowly ran her hands over the intricately carved flowers on the door and knew without a doubt that the workmanship was Nilan's. He had a gift with wood and stone.

Upon opening the cabinet, Elina found it to be stocked with wheat, dried fruit, corn, spices, and emergency candles and blankets.

My husband is always prepared, she thought. She touched the blankets a moment before closing the cabinet. She was stepping back when she felt a light breeze on her feet. It was coming from beneath the cabinet. She knelt down and leaned her head against the floor and saw a thin crack

almost as wide as the back of the cabinet. Curiosity got the best of her. She stood and pushed against the side of the cabinet. It was very heavy, but she managed to move it inch by inch. When she had pushed it far enough away, she gasped. She had uncovered a hidden doorway.

Elina retrieved the candle from the table and stood in front of the doorway. The breeze still blew, but not hard enough to put out the candle. Not wanting to take any chances on being trapped

in the dark, she went and picked up the lantern she'd spied in the corner and quickly lit it. She adjusted the wick and set the candle on the table. She took a deep breath and went back to the doorway. She was grateful to have something to divert her thoughts of Nilan being in danger, if only for a few moments. She held the light out in front of her and descended a set of stairs before finding herself on the flat earth. She stopped and looked around her.

It was a tunnel. The ceiling was low and Elina had to bend slightly as she walked. She didn't know how far the tunnel went, but the path was clear so she kept going, hoping she wouldn't abruptly hit a wall. After a while she began to smell the fresh scent of the sea, yet she knew she couldn't have possibly walked that far. Her flight with Nilan had not been long, but it was definitely longer than her walk. She was close enough to smell it, though.

A few yards ahead she saw a dim light coming from around a large rock and suddenly realized that this was an escape tunnel. Even though Nilan had never had any trouble, he'd still been prepared, and she was grateful for that. She stopped. There was no need for her to go further.

As thoughts of her husband being in danger quickly entered her mind once more, she turned and headed back.

J. Adams

Thirteen

An Unexpected Ally

Nilan climbed one of the tall trees and quietly waited for the enemy to appear. Deciding his bow and arrows wouldn't be necessary at the moment, he positioned his blowgun and readied himself. Inchants were a peaceful people and never resorted to violence unless absolutely necessary.

Nilan's home was being threatened and now that he had a wife to protect, the threat had doubled. He valued Elina above all else. He would give his life to keep her safe. She had been through so much already and as long as he was alive, no harm would come to her. He had promised her that. He also promised that he would come back to her. He intended to keep that promise.

Nilan readied himself as his ears picked up the sound of approaching footsteps.

* * *

Everything in Gin's gut told him this was not right. Thenoch's way was not the way. He'd known this for a long time, but he had been too concerned for his family and his own life to refuse Thenoch's orders. Gin realized now that he was a coward. So much blood had been shed at his hands because of his cowardice.

He paused by a tree and a strong bout of guilt washed over him.

This Inchant has done nothing wrong, he thought. *He saved a life, giving no thought to his own. He had to have known this would happen, yet he saved the girl anyway.* He sheathed his sword and pushed the helmet from his head.

"What in the blazes are you doing?" the man to his right whispered. The rest were still some distance behind them.

Gin raised himself to his full height, which made

him tower over the man and answered. "I am finished. I will most likely lose my life in this forest, but I will no longer be Thenoch's mercenary, shedding innocent blood."

"You coward!" the man hissed, pressing a fist against a tree, unaware of the sudden withering of its leaves.

"This is true," Gin agreed, "but I would rather be labeled a coward and die than take another innocent life."

The man glared at Gin. "We are all going to die this day anyway. I would rather die in battle than risk the lives of my family."

"I intend to die in these woods as well, but I will not lift my sword in Thenoch's name again."

"Then it will not be the Inchant's hand you die by, it will be mine."

Gin raised his eyes as the warrior lifted his sword.

Nilan's strong hearing allowed him to hear every word between the two men. Unbelievably, there was actually another human who was able to see through the lies of Thenoch. He had determined that there were no decent humans left in Dominae. Listening to the man's words, Nilan now knew he was wrong. This knowledge brought gladness to his heart.

With quick and silent agility, he moved through the tree tops until the two men were within view. He saw the determination in the large warrior's face and heard the angry words of the other man's reply. Then he saw the shorter man raise his sword.

Unable to move fast enough, Gin closed his eyes and braced himself for the blade to fall on him, but what happened next took him by complete surprise. His attacker suddenly dropped his sword and fell to the ground. He landed on his face and Gin saw the blow dart protruding from his neck. He frantically looked around him. Then he heard a powerful voice coming from the trees.

"Peace. I wish you no harm."

Gin sighed deeply, but his eyes were still ever-moving, trying to find the source of the voice.

"Nor I you," he finally said. "But there are others who do."

"How many?" The voice sounded closer.

"Ten."

"Including yourself?"

By now the voice was very close. Gin tried to remain calm. "No . . . but I have no wish to be included."

"Then you are no longer my enemy."

Gin startled. Out of nowhere the Inchant appeared. He instantly lowered his head. "No, my

lord, I am no longer an enemy to you." He closed his eyes as the being drew closer. When he felt a firm hand on his shoulder, he quickly opened his eyes.

"I am not a lord. I am Nilan, an Inchant warrior. Nothing more."

Gin finally raised his eyes to Nilan's. "I thank you for my life." He looked back through the trees. "They are not far. Their order is to kill you."

"Then we must prepare to greet them."

Fourteen

Quiet Thunder

Nilan repositioned himself in the tree. He looked in Gin's direction. The warrior was hiding behind a tree a hundred yards away. Nilan positioned his bow and waited. A couple of minutes later, the men began to trickle in. With lightening speed, Nilan's arrow sliced through the air hitting one man square in the chest. Before another five seconds had passed he took out five more men. The rest began to turn back, but one by one they all fell, each man with an arrow sticking in his back. Nilan made a mental count of the men and again scanned the area.

There was still one missing.

Gin startled as a knife whizzed passed the bridge of his nose and lodged in the tree he was standing next to. He turned toward the fast approaching figure while simultaneously pulling the knife from the tree. As the man drew his sword, Gin threw the knife. In the fraction of a second it was buried in the man's chest and he fell.

Gin released a deep breath and steadied himself. He definitely had not seen that one coming. He looked up in the tree at Nilan and his brow furrowed.

Nilan raised his hands and shrugged, smiling slightly. "My aim was fixed on him just in case, however, I knew your skills would be sufficient."

Gin scowled, then smiled slightly. "Your confidence is comforting."

Nilan laughed and Gin shook his head. Siding with this god-like being was indeed going to be an experience.

Hearing a low rumbling, Nilan and Gin looked

over where the man had fallen. Gin's eyes widened as the ground around the fallen man opened and swallowed him, then closed over him.

"Did . . . did that happen to the rest?"

"I am sure it did," Nilan responded.

"But how . . ."

Nilan answered before Gin could finish. "It is the forest's response to evil, and now that evil has entered, it is only a matter of time until the land here begins to change as well."

"You mean that is why Dominae has changed so? The evil of men?"

"That is why."

Gin's earlier guilt suddenly multiplied tenfold.

"Do not look back," Nilan said, reading his expression. "We cannot change what has passed. We can only deal with now and ponder what will be should Thenoch not be stopped."

Elina's heart began to pound violently as she heard the scrape of the bed against the floor and then the creak of the door opening above her. She wanted to rush up and greet Nilan, but what if it wasn't him? She eased back into a dark corner and pressed her back against the hard wall. Light streamed down as the door opened.

"*Sashana*, it is me."

Elina released a relieved sigh when she heard her husband's voice. In the next instant she was in his arms.

"I was so worried for you," she said, tightening her arms around his neck. "I was so afraid."

He held her close. "No need to fear for me, *sashana*. I will always come back to you."

Elina sighed and took comfort in Nilan's words.

He moved back slightly and took her shoulders in his hands. "My love, we have a guest."

"A guest?" she questioned. "Whatever do you mean?"

"It seems we have an unexpected ally," he said, taking her hand and leading her up the stairs.

Fifteen

The Guest

Nilan pulled the bed back over the door and took Elina to the kitchen where he left Gin waiting with a metal goblet of cool water. He felt her body trembling and placed his arm around her.

It is all right, he mentally crooned. *This man is a friend to us. He brings no danger.*

The two entered the kitchen and Gin immediately stood.

"Gin, this is my wife, Elina." He saw the surprise in the man's eyes.

"It is a pleasure to meet you," Gin said, bowing

slightly.

"And you," Elina said back, her voice hinting of wariness.

Gin looked back to Nilan. "So you married her, then? But . . . how?"

Nilan smiled, understanding his confusion. "True, the body chemistry of my people is very different, but still compatible with that of humans."

Gin looked thoughtful. "I wish you both every happiness, though you may be hard pressed to find it in the times to come."

Nilan understood the gravity of his words. He gestured to the table and they sat down. Gin reclaimed his seat and Elina stayed close to Nilan's side. He held her hand and looked directly into Gin's eyes. "Tell me of Thenoch's plan."

Gin leaned forward. "Well, simply put, he plans to put an end to you and take back what he considers his."

Nilan felt Elina tense and he squeezed her hand again, wanting to reassure her that he would keep her safe. "That will never be," he said, holding Elina's eyes with his. "Elina is my wife. Thenoch has no claim on her and he will never even breathe the same air as she. Neither will he take my life. There is an appointed time for every life force to end. Now is not mine."

"But how can you be so sure?" Elina asked, emotion cracking her voice.

Nilan pressed a hand to her face. "I cannot say how I know, *sashana*, only that I do." He turned back to Gin. "I know of Thenoch's character, but tell me more of the people. Surely there must be others like you. Others who are willing to stand up against him and fight for the right to live I peace."

Gin sighed. "Besides my wife and son, three possibly, maybe four, but I doubt you could find more. These are perilous times and Thenoch's stronghold grows more each day. Right is made to look wrong. Charity is frowned upon and selfishness is commended. He hates with a passion that is beyond description and his insidiousness knows no bounds." He paused, tugging a hand back through his mussed hair. "I sent my family away for their safety. I told them that if I have not come for them in two days to travel on to Anglann. It will be a longer trip traveling around the city, but I can see no other way. It pains me to admit it, but deep down I know there truly is no safe place."

Nilan felt his new friend's sudden sadness. He turned to look into Elina's eyes and her compassionate gaze answered his silent question. His eyes moved back to Gin. "Tell me where your family is and I will deliver them safely here to you." He squeezed Elina's hand and she smiled. "Our home is not large, but it is comfortable and there is enough room for you and your family. You are welcome here."

Gin's eyes were filled with both awe and disbelief. "You know nothing about me, yet you are willing to help me and my family?"

"You knew nothing about me, yet you chose to abandon Thenoch's orders and warn me. I am now privileged to know another good and honest human. Surely there are more. And with your help, we will find them and fight the evil that has spread."

"But how? Even if we do manage to find a few people that haven't sold their souls to Thenoch, we will never have enough to fight him."

Nilan was thoughtful for a moment. "Do you know of the war that was fought ten years ago between Krisandor and Jubilus?"

"Barely. When Thenoch came here and created Dominae, he forbade the people who followed him from that part of the world to ever speak of his old kingdom. We never really heard the details of the war, only that Ubal lost. Thenoch said it was because Ubal was weak." He paused and pulled up the sleeve of his tunic, exposing a patch of scaly skin. "As were we all. Though each of us still wears a brand on our skin, I and a couple of others, including my wife, recently chose to no longer indulge in Splendorfire. My thoughts have become clearer and there seems to be more clarity in my vision."

Nilan studied the brand for a moment. "I am puzzled," he said. "Since a branded woman cannot carry a child, how did you have a son?"

Gin smiled somewhat sadly. "He is not the son of our blood, but the son of our hearts. We found him when he was very young, homeless and alone. We took him into our home and he became a son to us."

"I see."

"The few people who came from the distant land of Anglann stayed unbranded for as long as they could. Then one by one they began to lose their lives in the fight to stay that way." Gin looked at Elina sadly. "I truly regret my part in it." The memory of the day he helped to raid her family's home etched deep lines of pain in his face, making him suddenly look older.

Elina's eyes were filled with compassion as she looked at him. "I hold nothing against you. I learned long ago that hatred only begets hatred."

The man nodded, his face holding an expression of deep contrition. Then he looked back at the Inchant warrior.

"Nilan," Gin said directly, "we may make this great effort, but to what end? From what I now understand, Krisandor was a great kingdom, and though there were not as many inhabitants there as there was in Jubilus, their number was still ten thousand times greater than our mere five or six, if that many."

Nilan smiled. "Actually it was twenty times greater, however the women and children remained in their homes."

Gin couldn't help but smile back. "I stand corrected. Twenty times our mere five or six."

Nilan stood and moved around the table, and

placed his hand on Gin's shoulder. "Before I found Elina, I was leaving this place behind, because I found no reason to stay. All I could see was evil. I did not think there was one decent soul in Dominae. I was wrong." He squeezed his shoulder. "You must believe, my friend, as I now do. I have found that all things are possible if we believe."

Sixteen

Fear And Loathing

While Gin told Nilan the location of his family, Elina prepared the two extra sleeping rooms for their guests and tried not to fret about her husband's safety as he undertook this task. He was used to flying while carrying extra weight and he assured her that carrying two people would not be a problem for him. Knowing this, Elina assumed she must have been as light as a feather to him when he carried her on their journey back to the forest.

After looking over the rooms a final time, Elina went in search of her husband. She found him in the

side courtyard giving Gin some last minute instructions on keeping her safe while he was gone,
even though it would only be a short while. She gave Gin a grateful smile as he walked away to give them some privacy. Nilan opened his arms and she moved into them.

Elina circled her arms around his neck, pressed her face in the curve of it and tangled her fingers in his soft, golden hair.

"Please be careful, Nilan," she whispered, tears burning her closed eyes. "I would die if anything happened to you."

"I will always come back to you, *sashana*," he whispered against her ear. "Remember that." He took her face between his hands and kissed her. "I love you."

"I love you," she said back, finally releasing him. "And I will be here waiting for your return."

* * *

Thenoch sat at a long wooden table in his private dining chamber and filled his plate with servings of the various dishes of food placed before him. Two servants stood by the door eagerly awaiting his beckoning like dogs waiting for attention from their master. He looked at them and smiled. He had trained them well.

There was a knock at the door and one of the servants opened it. Lucius timidly entered. When he reached the end of the table he bowed low.

"Master."

"What is it, my spineless little man?" he asked bitingly before shoving a slice of an apple into his deformed mouth.

Lucius bowed his head slightly, not daring to look his master in the eyes, a weakness that Thenoch thrived upon.

"A report from the guards posted outside the forest entrance. All twelve men report that none of the warriors have returned. We can only assume they are dead."

"You are not in a position to assume anything, half-wit!" he suddenly yelled, causing Lucius to cower. Then his voice became smooth and condescending. "Though you are most likely right." He stabbed his fork into a large piece of meat that was so undercooked, dark blood still oozed from it. He took a bite, allowing the blood to drip down his chin onto his red silk robe. It was another full minute before he spoke again.

"Tell the guards they are to remain at their posts. If there is any movement at all, they are to attack first and ask questions later."

"Yes, master."

"And one more thing," Thenoch said, pointing a bony finger. "Send three men to Gin's house. Tell them to take his wife and son into custody and lock them in the tower."

"Yes, master." Lucius bowed once more and left Thenoch to his meal.

Seventeen

Unlikely Target

The moon cast a haunted glow over the landscape. The red made the flecks in the snow shimmer like a sea of rare rubies. Nilan scanned the area and quickly landed at his destination. To the human eye there was nothing but snow-covered desolation, but Gin had told Nilan exactly what to look for and his eyes had zeroed in on the object from the skies.

A large, flat rock covered an opening to a hidden underground shelter. A small cottage had once sat atop the shelter, but it was destroyed long ago. Thenoch wanted all of his people where he could see them and the cottage was too far away from town. Needless to say, the elderly couple that

resided there were given an offer they couldn't refuse and moved to town.

Nilan knelt in the snow and slowly moved the rock away. It was dark inside the shelter–and quiet. However, his sight allowed him to see in the dark. He cautiously leaned over the hole, but no

objects were within view.

"Misha, Laslow," he called softly. "I am a friend. I was sent by your husband to find you."

Silence.

Nilan tried again. "I come in peace. You need not fear me. I have come to rescue you, to take you to your husband."

Silence.

Hoping no one else had gotten to them first, Nilan tried once more.

"Misha, Laslow, I am Nilan, an Inchant warrior. Gin sent me to bring you to him. He is at my home in Iskin Forest. He is safe. I have come to bring you to safety as well."

Nilan stayed silent and listened for a moment. He could hear them now. He could hear them breathing. He knew they were afraid to show themselves.

"Please trust me," he implored softly.

"Tell me true," a soft but shaky feminine voice called from the dark hole. "You are truly a friend to my husband?"

Nilan heaved an inward sigh of relief. "Yes, I am a friend to Gin, and to you and your son as well."

There was another moment of silence. Then came a male voice.

"We are coming out."

Nilan moved back and waited.

A red-headed young man slowly emerged from the hole. When he was out, he reached down to help his mother. Each of them had a small bundle of personal items strapped to their backs. Though they were both dusty and a light layer of dirt covered their faces, Nilan could still see her youthful beauty and his rough attractive features.

"Father has told us stories," Laslow said. "And I have heard a few from others, but I . . . I did not truly believe you were real." He smiled in wonder. "My lord, we are grateful to you for coming for us," He extended his hand.

Nilan gripped it firmly. "It is an honor. And as I told your father, I am not a lord, just an Inchant warrior."

Misha looked about her, noticing the few close tracks in the snow from Nilan's landing. She raised her eyes to him in awe and studied his massive wings for a moment. "How will . . . how will you . . ."

Nilan knew what she wanted to ask. Her puzzlement was clearly written in her expression. "I am strong enough to carry you both. You need only hold on." He knelt and replaced the rock, covering it with snow afterwards. Straightening, he stretched out his arms and gestured for them to

come to him. Each took a side and Nilan wrapped his arms around them. He told them both to put their arms around his neck and hold on. Then he extended his wings.

"Are you ready?" he asked softly, wanting to bring calmness to both of them.

Laslow nodded wordlessly, while his mother just stood looking frightened.

Nilan looked into her eyes. "You can trust me, Misha. I will not let you fall."

Finally giving a hint of a nod, she tightened her arms around his neck and took a deep breath. "I want to be with my husband. I am ready."

Nilan nodded, and with a flap of his wings they began to ascend. He heard them both gasp softly as their feet left the ground and thought of how different this would be than flying with Elina. He wasn't in any discomfort–it was just different. Flying with Elina had been heaven. He supposed it was because he had been in love with her even then.

Laslow looked down at the swiftly passing landscape in wonder, while Misha kept her eyes closed and her face pressed against Nilan's chest.

It wasn't long before the dark city came into view and Nilan ascended higher, though not as high as he had with Elina. Feeling Misha trembling, he didn't think she could handle it if he went any higher. He again smiled as he thought of Elina's soft warmth in his arms as they flew that day above the clouds. She had been so trusting, so vulnerable, completely dependent upon him, and it had felt good giving her a permanent place in his heart. It felt good to be needed by someone–someone who had changed him so completely.

Thoughts of his wife waiting for him urged him to quicken his speed. He needed to see her, to be with her, to touch her and hold her in his arms again.

Just as he was about to reach the forest, Nilan jerked. An instant burning sensation seized his shoulder. He momentarily squeezed his eyes shut against the pain.

Laslow's eyes widened in horror as they fell on the arrow protruding from Nilan's shoulder. It had just barely missed his own. He felt the sudden change in altitude and looked at his mother as she began to weep.

Nilan struggled to pull up, mentally calling upon strength he'd never had to use before.

Laslow again looked into his mother's eyes. "We are not going to make it."

Elina was sitting by the fireplace in their room reading when a powerful sensation seized her, gripping at her heart to the point that she suddenly found it hard to breathe. The book fell from her hands onto the floor. As she closed her eyes and began taking deep breaths, her thoughts shot to Nilan and her chest tightened.

"No, no, no," she moaned. She stood and staggered from the room, leaning against the hallway wall.

"Gin!" she shrieked. "Gin!"

Gin appeared from nowhere. "What is it, Elina?" His voice was bordering panic.

She looked into his eyes as tears spilled down her cheeks. "It is Nilan. Something has happened!"

The cloaked archer swiftly entered the royal chamber. He pushed the hood away from his shaved head and knelt before Thenoch's throne. There was great pride in his eyes and triumph in his countenance.

"Master, my arrow hit its target."

Thenoch smiled widely, his gruesome face

appearing even more sinister. "Well done. Now, go and retrieve my prize."

"And what is your will for Gin's wife and son?"

Gin had betrayed him, and there was only one way to handle traitors. If you cannot not kill them, then you hit them where it hurts.

"Kill them both."

Eighteen

Strength

A thick layer of clouds moved over the moon. The stars were also shrouded in darkness. Despite his wounded shoulder, Nilan managed to keep Misha and Laslow from slipping into the dark abyss of the forest and was able to stay airborne. He was in a great deal of pain, but his senses were still strong. After flying for what seemed like forever, he reached the area above his home and began his shaky descent.

By the time Nilan's feet touched the courtyard ground he was sweating. He needed to get the arrow out so that he could begin healing. Since the wound was not fatal, he would heal fast. While it would take a human weeks to completely heal from such a wound, it would take an Inchant less than a day.

Misha and Laslow both heaved great sighs of relief, grateful to have made it. Nilan asked them if they were all right. They nodded and he gestured for them to go in. Gin was already on the other side of the door and Misha immediately flew into his arms followed by Laslow. Gin hugged them both with fierceness and kissed his wife over and over.

"Nilan!" Elina cried, pushing by the three. She stopped short of flinging herself against him when she saw the arrow protruding from his shoulder. "Oh, Nilan," she choked.

"I am all right," he soothed, pulling her close to his uninjured side. He pressed a kiss to her forehead and then her ear and whispered, "*Eitomilay, sashana.* It will be all right."

Tears continued to streak her cheeks. "I was so worried. I . . ." Her voice broke and she couldn't finish.

"Shhh," he soothed. "All will be well."

Gin's voice was guilt-riddled as he said, "I am so sorry, Nilan."

"No need to apologize," Nilan assured him. "Elina, this is Misha and Laslow."

"Pleased to meet you," Elina said.

"We are very pleased to meet you as well," Misha said.

Elina drew forth a smile of acknowledgment and quickly turned her attention back to Nilan.

Nilan glanced down at his blood-soaked sleeve. "Please excuse me," he said to their guests. "I need to tend to my wound."

"Allow me to help," Gin offered. "It is the least I can do after everything you have done."

"That will not be necessary," Elina said. "I will assist my husband." She looked into Nilan's eyes and opened her thoughts to him. *It is my place.*

Nilan marveled at her bravery and devotion. "Come then, *sashana.*"

She nodded and took his arm.

"Nilan," Misha called as the husband and wife started down the hallway. "Thank you for saving us."

Nilan smiled. "You are most welcome. Gin will show you to your rooms. Please, make yourselves comfortable."

J. Adams

Nineteen

Breakdown

Once Elina had placed everything she needed on the kitchen table and Nilan had shed his tunic, she began the task of removing the arrow from Nilan's shoulder. She tried to keep her emotions under control, but with each grunt that escaped Nilan, a fresh stab of pain pricked her heart as well. He told her what to do and bravely sat while she cut into his flesh around the arrow.

His blood completely covered her hands and they became so slippery that at one point the knife slipped and made a small slit in her finger. Nilan asked her if she was all right and she assured him she was. The cut burned, but she ignored it, determined to get the arrow out of her husband's arm and get the wound sewn up as quickly as possible.

At last, the arrow was out. Elina cleaned the wound thoroughly, stitched it up, and dressed it. Then she cleaned up the bloody mess. Finally, she wrapped the cut on her finger. Nilan admired her handiwork on his shoulder and commended her on her skills, but she didn't hear him. Now that he was on his way to healing, the emotion she'd been holding back finally forced its way to the surface.

Elina stood staring down at the being that she loved more than life, and all she could think about at that moment was how close she had come to losing him. A little further over in his chest and the arrow could have claimed his life. He would have been taken from her.

And she would have died, too.

"*Sashana*," Nilan said when Elina continued to stand like a stone statue, silently staring at him. She did not answer.

He stood and touched her face. "Elina." He was

preparing to enter her thoughts when she finally spoke.

"I could have lost you." Her voice was barely a whisper.

"No, *sashana*. You will never lose me."

Her tears began again. "I felt it . . . when you were hurt. You . . . you could have been . . ." She didn't finish. She pressed a hand over her mouth, suddenly nauseous."

"You felt it?" Nilan asked, bewildered. "But . . . how?"

Elina shook her head, not able to speak. She quickly turned and ran out the kitchen door. Making it to the edge of the garden, she leaned over and lost the contents of her stomach. Nilan was at her side, rubbing her back. She was about to tell him she was all right, but the nausea rose again, causing her to heave once more.

"*Sashana*." Nilan's voice broke.

Hearing the anguished emotion in his voice, Elina tried to assure him she would be okay.

"Come. We must get you to bed. You have endured much today and . . . I am so sorry."

Elina finally turned to him and said with hoarse

emotion, "This is nothing compared to what I would have had to endure had I lost you."

Nilan pulled her close and kissed her temple. "Come, my love." He took her hand and led her into the house to their room. He left her to change into her sleeping tunic and went to check on their guest. After making sure Gin and his family had everything they needed, he returned to his wife.

Elina was now calm and lying in bed. When Nilan slipped beneath the covers and extinguished the lamp, she moved into his arms and never wanted to leave them again. She lay quietly, listening to the easy rhythm of his heart and thanked the heavens for the marvelous sound. Though Nilan had returned to her and was healing, she knew their trials were far from over. They were just beginning.

A tear rolled over the bridge of her nose and landed on Nilan's smooth chest. When he felt it, he held her tighter and she burrowed into him. Her tired voice softly filtered through the silence.

"What shall we do?"

His answer was in his own language. He buried his face in her hair and continued to speak the soothing words, the musical tone of his voice rich and deep.

Elina didn't understand the words he spoke, but she felt the comfort they wrought and after a short while fell into a dreamless slumber.

When Elina finally drifted to sleep, Nilan silently let the tears come. He couldn't believe it. Elina had felt his pain.

She felt it!

She had known he was in trouble. How could it be? How could they be so connected? The bond between two Inchant mates was strong, but Elina was human. This should not be. Yet it was, and if such a thing were possible, it made her all the more precious to him.

"What do you mean you couldn't find him!" Thenoch roared.

Any other warrior would have cowered beneath Thenoch's wrath, but not the archer. He stood straight and tall, never moving his eyes away from his leader's.

"It seems the Inchant made it into the forest after all."

Thenoch leaned back in his chair and silently studied the warrior for a moment. He took in the heavy, dark cloak that draped his massive shoulders. His shaved head sat atop a thick neck, and his arms and legs were the size of those of two men. He was a loner. Always had been. When Thenoch inquired about why he wasn't married, the man roughly told him that there was not enough room in his life for gentility and ambition. The man was insolent and did not frighten easily. Surprisingly, Thenoch liked that about him. He was different from the other cowardly soldiers in his service.

Even still, Thenoch realized that those attributes made him a dangerous man. He would surely watch him more closely.

"So, Brutin, my brave warrior, what do you suggest we do now?"

Brutin smiled. "We wait and watch. Let him

sweat for a day. Then we storm the forest and kill them all. Gin, his wife, his son, and the Inchant. And then we will bring the girl to you."

Thenoch smiled darkly. "I rather like this plan. A good one indeed."

"I thought it would please you."

"But first," Thenoch added, "I have another small plan of my own."

The meenabird's loud caw rang out in the darkened sky.

Nilan awakened and exited the cottage, having heard the call. He gazed up into the dark sky.

The moon was now veiled, but he was still able to make out the creature as it dropped a leather-bound scroll through the trees. Lifting his uninjured arm, Nilan caught the scroll with little effort.

There was no question who the message was from. He looked up again at the bird as it hovered above, as if it were waiting but dared not come down into the forest. He took the scroll inside and headed towards the kitchen, but Elina met him in the hallway, having awakened when he got up.

"What is it?" she whispered, not wanting to wake their guests.

"It is a message from Thenoch."

When Elina's eyes widened, he squeezed her hand. "Come," he said and they went back to their room and sat on the bed. Feeling her eyes on him, he unrolled the scroll and silently read, his brow furrowing and the frown lines deepening with each word he read. He finally looked up at her.

"He has informed me that if I bring you to him, both our lives will be spared."

Before Elina turned her tearful gaze downward, Nilan saw the guilt in her eyes. He opened his mind to hers and reached out and lifted her chin.

"No, *sashana*. This is not your fault."

Elina closed her eyes as tears fell down her cheeks. "If you had not brought me here . . ."

"He cannot hurt us," Nilan interrupted, taking her hands in his, trying to send her strength.

"But there is only the two of us, and Gin and his family. Maybe I should just . . ."

No, he said to her mind before she could finish. *I will not take you to him. You are mine, Elina. Mine. He has no claim on you.*

Elina couldn't help the guilt she felt at the coming danger. If Nilan had not brought her back, he would be safe. If he had not stopped to help her, he would be safe with his people in Krisandor. Looking into her husband's eyes and searching her own heart, she could never regret their love or being his wife, but she still felt guilty.

"We will not be alone," he said, caressing her cheek. "It may seem that way now, but we are not alone in this. We never will be."

Elina sighed and forced a smile and nodded, taking comfort in his words.

"Now," Nilan said, pulling back the covers for her to get back into bed, "I have a reply to send."

Thenoch's red eyes narrowed as he read the scroll. He tossed it across the throne room, just barely missing the meenabird perched near the window, bringing a loud squawk from the creature, still tired from its flight. He gripped the golden arms of the chair and seethed, cursing out loud. Then he calmed, his behavior becoming more erratic with each passing day.

"No matter," he said to no one. "I will have her soon enough." His hands formed fists as he thought of Nilan. "And you, my winged friend, will rue the day you took my prize."

Twenty

Bound By Blood

Elina awakened the next morning to find Nilan gone and she began to panic. She was about to get up and go in search of him when their room door opened and he entered, carrying a breakfast tray.

"Good morning, *sashana.*"

She heaved a deep sigh of relief as he placed the tray in the middle of the bed and climbed back in. He leaned over and kissed her. "Did you sleep well?"

"I did," Elina replied with a smile, grateful for his nearness. "But what of you? We were up late and there was not much time to rest your shoulder. Did it cause you much pain?"

Nilan smiled and began moving the joints of his arm around. "I had no pain. It has healed even faster than I anticipated, which means it must not have been as bad as it seemed."

"For that, I am thankful."

"As am I."

The two began eating their breakfast of fruit, cheese, and slices of meat left over from the day before.

"How are our guest faring this morning?" Elina asked him.

"They are well rested and having breakfast."

"I should be up to taking care of them. What must they think of me?" Her first guest and she had been a terrible hostess.

Nilan reached for her hand. "They think you are an adoring wife who exhausted herself tending to her husband's needs." He lifted her hand and kissed it. "I am prompted to agree." He noticed the loosened bandage on her finger. "We should replace this."

"Hmmm. It feels fine," Elina said removing the small piece of cloth. If not for the bandage, she wouldn't have remembered the cut at all. "That's strange," she said, turning her finger over and back a couple of times. "It is gone."

"What do you mean?" Nilan said, taking her hand again and examining her finger. He looked over her whole hand, then her finger again.

Elina noticed his perplexed expression. "I was very distraught last night. Perhaps the cut was not as bad as I had supposed."

"Indeed, there was a great deal going on." He made a contemplative noise and checked her fingers once more. "Perhaps you are right." He smiled and touched her face, and she leaned into his caress, never tiring of his warmth.

"I am so grateful you are all right," Elina said with strength. She leaned over the tray and kissed him again, pressing her fingers in his golden tresses.

"You will never lose me, Elina," he whispered, deepening the kiss. After another moment, he cleared his throat and eased back. "Our guest are waiting," he said with a smile.

"Oh, right," she said as color crept into her cheeks and he chuckled.

They quickly finished their breakfast. Then Elina

changed and they went to join Gin and his family.

Thenoch stood on the balcony of his enormous sleeping chamber and watched the men below as they suited up in their armor and readied themselves for the raid on Iskin Forest. There were five hundred of them, and the purpose of their very existence was to do his bidding. Before the day was over, Nilan would be dead, and he would have his prize back.

He smiled as he thought of Elina. Despite her belligerence and hatred of him, there was not a more beautiful creature in all of Dominae. Something so beautiful should not be free to roam wild, but should be owned–possessed.

Thenoch's power had gotten him everything he has ever wanted and more. Everything that is . . . except Elina. He didn't just want Elina's allegiance and obedience. He wanted *her*. He wanted her complete and unquestionable devotion. He had wanted this since the first moment he laid eyes on her.

And today he would have it. Before the day was

over, she would pledge herself to him. The sound of Brutin's voice below broke through his thoughts.

"All right, men, get into formation!"

Thenoch watched as the five hundred men formed lines and rows, their movements reminding him of pieces on a game board, which is exactly what they were to him. Like seasoned warriors, they were orderly and precise in their movement into position. They were very skilled in the art of warfare and trained for the instant kill.

He smiled. *Yes, today, victory will be mine.*

Just as the men were set to begin their march of war, a distant humming touched their ears. Brutin and his men began to look around, puzzled by the sound. Gradually the humming turned into a drumming which grew louder with each passing second.

"Hold your position," Brutin called as the men began to be agitated.

Suddenly the sky began to darken as if a violent rainstorm was upon them. Only it wasn't rain. The men looked toward the sky and froze in both fear and terrible awe. Brutin's demeanor quickly changed, and though for a brief second his eyes held a bit of surprise, thrown off guard by what he was witnessing, his stone face remained expressionless. He looked up toward the balcony at Thenoch, whose face had completely paled, making him look even more like the walking dead. The eyes of each man were glued to the skies, some of them cowering, some of them standing like statues with open mouths, unable to believe what they were seeing.

Above them were thousands of Inchants, so many that the sky seemed to be covered in gold. Their bodies seem to shimmer as they passed over the city, their hair rippling behind them like spun
gold. The winged beings were all headed toward Iskin Forest. The men continued to watch, the gold
blanketing the heavens seeming endless.

After another moment the sky was finally clear and had returned to its usual dreariness. Brutin
took in the various expressions of fear on the faces of his men and grunted before looking up toward
Thenoch once more. Studying this new fear in the master's eyes, he deduced that the raid would definitely be on hold for now.

Nilan felt them approaching before they were even close to the city. He, Elina, Gin, Misha, and Laslow were sitting around the dining table discussing their plans when Nilan heard the low humming. Then, one by one the others began to hear it, too. Nilan's blood began to coarse through his veins with force.

His people were coming.

He grabbed Elina's hand and quickly went out to the courtyard. The others followed. Nilan smiled and held tightly to his wife's hand and watched the skies in wonder.

Twenty-one

Family

Elina watched in what she could only exclaim as wondrous awe as the Inchant people began to descend from the gold-covered sky. Except for awakening in the cave and seeing Nilan, her eyes had never beheld such a marvelous sight. There were thousands of them, their descents stretching out all over the forest. She couldn't believe it. She turned her wide eyes to her husband.

"How . . . How did they know?"

Nilan smiled and gently pressed a hand to her face. "The connection of my people is strong, *sashana,* and the bond between family members is even stronger." He turned to the male and female that stood at the forefront of the massive crowd. He released Elina's hand and walked toward the two.

Elina watched the couple move forward and the three embraced.

"*Kitolimaki*," Nilan said as he closed his eyes and pressed a kiss to the woman's head. "How I have missed you, my sister."

"And I you," she said, pulling back slightly with a smile.

Nilan and the man gripped each other's arms firmly. The man grinned. "It is good to see you, my brother," he said.

"And you, Ansel," Nilan said back.

"By the look of things as we passed over the city, it seems we arrived just in time."

"For that, I am grateful." Nilan's eyes scanned the crowd of Inchants. "To all of you."

His acknowledgment was answered by his people as hands were raised and then fisted and pressed to their chest in the Inchant greeting.

Nilan turned and held a hand out to Elina where

she stood in the doorway of their home. "Come, *sashana*," he called.

Elina smiled and moved forward, taking his hand.

"Mazina, Ansel, this is my wife, Elina." He looked into Elina's eyes and smiled. "Elina, meet my sister and her husband."

Mazina smiled widely. She stepped forward and took Elina's hand. She had sensed her brother's happiness but wasn't clear on the source. Now she knew. "It is an honor and a pleasure to meet you," she said, squeezing Elina's hand. "You are very beautiful."

"Thank you," Elina said, blushing deeply. "I am honored to meet you as well. Nilan has told me much about you."

"Did he now?" Mazina said, smiling at her brother. "You must tell me what he has said sometime and I can tell you whether it is true or not."

Elina smiled. "I will."

Nilan put an arm around his wife's waist and looked from his sister to her husband, then let his eyes again scan his people. "Thank you again for coming. Now come. Let us plan and ready ourselves."

Twenty-two

The Plan

Krisandor

Cillian and Sakriel stood before the garden room window and looked out over the land, both of them deep in thought over the coming events. The king turned to his son and took in his traveling attire. The white, gold-trimmed tunic and leather leggings emphasized his muscular physique. His dark hair was pulled back and held in place with a leather tie. His green eyes were clear and determined.

"You are ready, then?"

"Yes, Father." He had again opened his mind and

called upon his extended gifts, and was now
ready for the change his body would undergo to travel
from kingdom to kingdom.

"Though the gate of Krisandor is permanently
shut, you must do what you can to help the few
who possess good hearts in Dominae. We must purge
that kingdom of evil and prepare those who choose to
listen for the coming change." Cillian paused, placing a
hand on Sakriel's shoulder. "When those with changed
hearts ask to come with you, you must make them
understand why the cannot. Once the evil is gone they
will need to stay in Dominae and rebuild. It will be a
happy place for them and every kingdom will live .in
peace."

Sakriel nodded. "The Inchants should be there
now."

"Yes," Cillian agreed.

"I am sure when this is over, Mazina's brother
will accompany them to Krisandor when they return."

"He will not be alone," Cillian said thoughtfully.

"No," Sakriel agreed with a smile. "He will not."

* * *

By evening, the Inchants had built shelters

throughout the forest. They gathered nuts and berries and flew to the shore and caught fish for their meals. They also inspected their weapons. Nilan told his people about Thenoch and his evil. They formed a plan of infiltration and prepared for Prince Sakriel's arrival, ready to assist him in every way possible.

Later, when his people had settled for the night, Nilan shared with Mazina and Ansel the details of finding Elina battered and half frozen in the snow. Holding his mate close to his side, he told them about the abuse she'd suffered at the hand of Thenoch, about caring for her in the cave, and how he had immediately lost his heart to her.

Mazina watched Elina's whole countenance glow with love for Nilan. It was as if the two were becoming one soul. She wondered how such a bond could be when Elina was human. How had they forged such a connection?

No matter, she thought. *My brother is happy, and I am content for him.*

Mazina suddenly stiffened and closed her eyes as she sensed a familiar presence. She opened them and smiled.

"Sakriel is here."

Twenty-three

The Arrival

Sakriel refused Nilan and Elina's offer to let him have their sleeping room. He also refused Gensal's family, choosing to take shelter with Mazina and Ansel.

Sakriel's coming had been one of wonder for all of them, and his appearance had left both Nilan and Elina speechless. Elina never had the privilege of seeing Prince Sakriel or his father before, but she'd heard of his kindness and goodness. She also knew the principles of the sacred scroll. Her parents taught them to her and she had never forsaken them. She would die first.

Elina never saw anything as amazing as Sakriel descending through the trees in the shimmering white and gold tunic to stand before them in the courtyard. It was pure magic and she felt the nobility that radiated from him. For the third time in her life, she was completely speechless. The first had been in the cave when she opened her eyes to the vision of the Inchant warrior standing

before her with his massive wings spread, who was now her husband. The second had been the arrival of his people.

Now, in the courtyard, Sakriel stood before them all and offered counsel and instruction.

"There is no need for me to tell you to stand ready. Your people are born to defend what is right. Tomorrow at dawn I will begin my work. Those who choose to listen will need your protection" He

paused, scanning the golden faces giving him their full attention. "We will sorrow for those who choose not to listen, just as we will for lives lost . . . but as my father counseled, it is the way of things. It must be."

Sakriel ended his counsel and the people retired for the night, leaving warriors to stand guard throughout the forest.

Inside, Elina made sure Gin and his family were settled before retiring to her sleeping room to wait for Nilan. She had been feeling a little lightheaded throughout the day, but it had progressively gotten worse and she welcomed this time of rest.

She wiped a hand across her wet brow. Her body was hot and clammy, and the sudden need to lie down overtook her before she could change into her sleeping tunic. She wondered what it could be since she'd never been sick in her life. Truthfully, she'd never known anyone who had been sick. Humans *don't get* sick.

She closed her eyes and lay there, wishing she could get up to open the window. Maybe the breeze would help her feel cooler. She tried but only made it to the edge of the bed before her legs gave out and she dropped to her knees and leaned over the side of the bed.

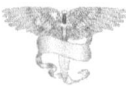

That was the way Nilan found her.

"Elina!" He quickly went to her, then lifted her and placed her on the bed. "What is it?"

Elina was completely weak. "I don't know," she answered.

Placing his hand on her arm, he felt the heat radiating from her skin before he even touched her. "You are burning up, *sashana*."

"I know." She tugged at her robe. "It is so hot, Nilan. I couldn't get to the window to open it." Her eyes hurt and it was hard for her to focus. But she did see the worry on her husband's face and tried to comfort him. "I will be all right, my love."

Nilan removed Elina's robe and pulled the thin covering over her, tucking it under her arms. He went to the kitchen and got a bowl of cold water and a cloth. Sitting next to her on the bed, he gently wiped the cool cloth over her pale face before placing it on her forehead, his whole being worried for her. He had never experienced illness himself and he had never known a human to be ill. He was beside himself wondering what he could do for her and it pained him to see her suffer in any way. After a while, Elina's body began to cool slightly, but she was still very warm. Nilan held her hand between his.

I am here, beloved, he silently voiced to her. *Be well for me*.

He was surprised when Elina opened her eyes and he squeezed her hand. She gave him a weak smile and his heart warmed. The color was returning to her cheeks.

"How are you feeling?" he asked, pressing a hand to her face.

"Tired," she sighed.

He caressed her cheek. "Then sleep, beloved," he said, leaning forward and pressing a kiss to her lips.

"Are you coming to bed?"

"Yes. I just need to speak with my sister a moment." He turned down the lamp, kissed her again and whispered, "I will be here soon. Just sleep."

Nilan met Mazina in the back courtyard. His eyes were intense.

"What is it?" she asked.

"It is Elina. Something is happening."

In the city a secret meeting was taking place in the war room of the palace. In attendance were Brutin, Lucius, and the thirty members of The Order. The men sat in ornately carved wooden chairs. Each of the warriors were of different height and build. Some had family. Some didn't. The armor of each man was worn, scratched, and dented and their eyes were set in grim determination. Each face wore the scars of battle. And all were completely loyal to Thenoch, who sat at the front of the room in a high-back, jewel-encrusted, golden chair.

Thenoch motioned for Brutin to stand. "What measures have you taken?"

Brutin's dark eyes were unwavering as he met Thenoch's stare. "My lord, fifty guards are posted on the outer perimeter of the forest. Some men are camped nearby and the rest are scattered throughout the city."

The dark lord nodded. "Keep the men in position. We will allow the Inchants a day to lower their guard. Then tomorrow when the blood moon rises, we will strike."

Nilan removed his tunic and leggings before slipping under the covers and gently taking his sleeping wife in his arms. Despite her body temperature feeling equal to his, she was trembling slightly. He held her close and she burrowed herself against him. Tucking the covers around them both, he heaved a relieved sigh when her trembling ceased. He took a deep breath and forced his body to relax while clearing all thoughts from his mind. At last, he began to slumber, his subconscious preparing him for what the coming morning would bring.

Twenty-four

Redeeming Love

Just before sunrise, Sakriel stood on the front step of the small shop on the edge of town. Twelve Inchants stood around the building as Sakriel had requested. The warrior's eyes were alert, their senses fine-tuned. Dressed in gold tunics and leather leggings, each warrior had a bow and quiver of arrows strapped to his back. Sakriel also wore a silver-trimmed, white tunic and gray leather leggings.

He knocked on the door and waited patiently. He knew it would take the occupant some time to get to the door. After another moment, the door opened.

"Esmarine, peace to you," Sakriel said softly.

The blind woman's eyes narrowed. "Who is it that wishes me peace?" She couldn't place the voice or the scent. It was different.

"A visitor from Krisandor."

Esmarine's filmy gray eyes widened, her wrinkled face filling with both confusion and wonder. "Well I'll be. How did you get here?"

Sakriel smiled. "How is not as important as why. And if you would permit me to enter and visit with you for a short while, I will give you that answer."

Just then, a gentle breeze touched the woman's face, bringing with it a familiar fragrance. She sniffed the air. "You have him with you," she stated, a subtle fear entering her voice.

"If you mean Nilan, no, he is not with me. However, a few of his people are here and will remain outside while we visit."

"His people!" she said as her eyes widened again. "You mean there are more of them here?"

"Many more," Sakriel answered patiently. "Now, may I enter, for what I shall tell you is of great importance."

Esmarine's wary eyes looked down for a moment in hesitation before she moved aside and let him enter. She led him to the back of the small shop where she lived.

Sakriel took in the small room with its simple wooden furniture, hanging plants, tapestry-covered floor, and small fireplace. Around the corner he glimpsed a small kitchen table. It was a cozy abode. He sat next to Esmarine on a cushioned bench and immediately began to explain whey he was
there. He told her of Thenoch's treachery. He knew she was already aware of most of this, but he needed to impress upon her the wickedness that now abounded at the hand of the dark lord and his minions. He told her of the evil effects of Splendorfire and the power Thenoch had over the people when they indulged.

"Esmarine, Thenoch can deceive you and have you believe that good is evil and evil is good. When you follow him, the line is blurred. You are led down a dark path and soon you begin to do things you never would, had you not partaken of the forbidden drink and given him power over you."

Sakriel watched Esmarine lower her head for a

moment. When she finally raised her eyes, he saw the sorrow in them.

"It is too late for me. I have done many things that I am now ashamed of." She closed her eyes, shook her head and repeated, "It is too late for me."

Sakriel smiled and reached for one of her gnarled hands. "It is not too late."

"How?" she asked, her sightless eyes searching.

"Trust me," he said softly. "If you truly desire to be free of Thenoch's influence, it is not too late." He looked at her eyes. "How did you lose your sight, Esmarine?"

The woman sighed, the lines in her tired, weathered face deepening. "Would you believe it started thirty years ago after my first taste of Splendorfire? The morning after consuming a goblet full, I awakened with a burning fever and a brand on my shoulder. The brand stopped spreading after a while, but the fever weakened my eyesight. Five years later I was completely blind." A tear rolled down one of the deep creases on her face.

Sakriel squeezed her hand. "Do you believe what I have told you today?"

Esmarine nodded. "I do."

"Will you vow to do no more evil and to choose what is noble and good?"

"I will," she answered with conviction.

He released her hand. "Close your eyes, Esmarine."

When her lids closed, Sakriel lightly placed his hands on them. "I promise that the goodness of your heart will shine through your eyes." He moved his hands away.

Esmarine slowly opened her eyes and gasped.

"I can see!"

Twenty-five

Changed

Nilan awakened at dawn to the cooing of doves. He heard the soft voices of his people echoing through the open window. With his eyes still closed, he tightened his arms around Elina and pressed his face into her hair, inhaling its sweetness.

Then he froze.

Drawing back slightly, he sucked in a breath and smiled as his awe-filled, teary gaze fell on his sleeping wife. The dark curls he so loved were gone, replaced by straight dark locks with generous streaks of gold. Her once fair skin now almost matched his own golden color. Her delicate arms were still delicate, but were now defined with lean muscle.

He had always thought she was beautiful, the most beautiful human he had ever seen, but now . . . now she nearly took his breath away. She was indescribably magnificent!

And she was his.

He'd concluded the night before what was happening, and he knew what had brought about the change. He discussed with Mazina Elina's exposure to his blood through the cut on her finger, and Mazina agreed it was possible. But he never could have guessed how incredible her transformation would be. In the history of the Inchant people, nothing like this had ever happened before.

Unable to resist waking her another moment, Nilan softly caressed Elina's cheek.

She slowly opened her eyes.

"What is it, my love?" Elina asked as she took in the look of joy and wonder she saw in Nilan's expression.

Instead of speaking, Nilan got up and took a silver hand mirror from the dresser. He sat down and handed it to her.

Elina looked at her reflection and her mouth fell open. She touched her face, her hair, then her face again. She put the mirror down and took in the light golden skin of her arms. She finally looked at Nilan.

"What has happened to me?" The question came out a whisper. She reached up and touched her husband's face and then her own again. She felt incredible strength surging through her. "How?"

Nilan smiled and caressed her cheek. "It seems we are indeed bound. My blood flows through you."

"But how?" She lifted her hand, turning it over and back again. "How?" she repeated.

He took her hand and answered, "It was the cut on your finger."

"The cut," she whispered. "But . . . it was so small."

"It was enough," he said with a smile. "When your cut disappeared, part of me wondered about it.

Then, when you became ill last night, I knew something was happening." He touched her face again. "And now look at you! Nothing like this has ever happened in the history of our people."

Elina moved her hands around to her back and found it unchanged. Part of her was relieved.

Reading her thoughts, Nilan said, "I do not think it will be a complete transformation. Our wings are present at birth."

She nodded and wondered anew at this new power surging through her–a power of well being, of clarity of thought–a perfect harmony of mind, body, and spirit. She had never experienced anything so exquisite. If she had to give it a name, should could not, for there were no words. Suddenly wondering how Nilan felt about the change in her, she opened her thoughts to his, the new strength of their mental connection taking her by surprise.

Does this disappoint you? Are your feelings for me changed?

Nilan drew her close and gazed longingly into her eyes. *Oh, beloved, can you not feel how my heart burns for you? Can you not see it in my eyes? You were, and still are, the most beautiful thing I have ever seen. You mean everything to me,* sashana. *Everything.*

Elina felt the truth of his words. She saw it in his eyes, felt it spoken from his soul to hers.

"It frightens me," he said close to her ear, "this powerful hold you have on me. Nothing has ever frightened me before, but this does. It is as if I never truly lived until you came into my life."

"I feel the same," she said with a teary smile.

Kilana etn intietalan, sashana," he whispered and kissed her.

Elina held him close and took hold of his words of love–words in the language she now understood completely.

Twenty-six

The Kindling

Lucius knelt before Thenoch's throne.

"Master, I have the most disturbing news!"

"What is it?" the dark lord said impatiently. He had a low tolerance for those who disturbed his meals.

The servant's voice was wary as he spoke again. "A visitor was at Esmarine's house. He was accompanied by Inchant warriors. I have never seen this man before."

Thenoch's red eyes narrowed. He knew of the man whom Lucius spoke. He'd felt Sakriel's presence the moment of his arrival. The feeling shook him to his bones.

He knew why the Great Prince was there–he knew his kingdom was at risk.

He knew King Cillian and his son would not be satisfied until they possessed Dominae as well. Thenoch was not about to let that happen. As long as there was breath in his body, Dominae would be his.

"I know what his plan is," Thenoch said at last. "However, I have a new plan of my own."

Sakriel worked tirelessly throughout the day. Besides Esmarine, he was only able to get through to five others, and at each of those homes he left a guard of twelve Inchants. The remaining citizens were under Thenoch's spell and would not betray him. If there was to be a war, they would fight for Thenoch, and die if they had to. Anything and everything the dark lord asked of them they would do. Thenoch was their god. They would have no other.

It pained Sakriel to see so many throwing away their lives, unwilling to bend or yield to the truth–not

Thenoch's truth, but a truth that was as old as time and would forever exist. And that truth was that good and evil could not coexist forever. One would have to yield, and evil surely would not be the victor. It could not.

Sakriel and his guard were heading back to the forest when a feeling came to him.

The sleeping giant has fully awakened.

He opened his mind to telepathic communication with the Inchant warriors standing guard at the homes of the six souls who had embraced the truth.

Take them to the forest–and prepare.

It is about to begin.

Twenty-seven

It Is Time

Mazina, Ansel, and a large group of Inchants stood around Nilan and Elina, amazed and awed at her transformation. Nilan answered their questions the best he could. He still found it a little hard to believe himself.

Elina smiled and squeezed his hand, warmed by his continuous gaze. His people were now her people. She was truly a part of him now She shared his blood and their souls were merged.

"A human Inchant," Elina had laughed and called herself. Nilan and Mazina decided that would not do, so they came up with a new name for what she had become. *Sashalimai*, which translated, literally meant "the beautiful changed one." Elina liked that name better.

She spent the morning in training with Nilan and the other Inchants and was now very skilled at the the bow and arrow, blowgun, and using a knife. Her hearing and vision had magnified and her other senses were overpowering at moments. She knew she wouldn't be quite as deadly as the rest, but she was aptly skilled enough to defend herself, her husband, and her people, and able to fight in the coming war.

While Nilan was both impressed and pleased with Elina's new abilities, he was still concerned for her safety. He planned to stay as close to her as possible.

Sakriel descended from the sky, followed by the six guards of Inchants, carrying the people who chose to abandon Thenoch's evil. He stood before them and opened his thoughts to theirs.

It is time.

Elina changed into Mazina's extra tunic and leggings. She took Misha, Esmarine, and the others to the hidden chamber beneath her sleeping room and instructed them to stay there. She showed them the escape tunnel should it become necessary to use it. After assuring them they would be safe, she recovered the entrance with the bed and went to rejoin Nilan. She was surprised to find him in the garden. His back was turned to her. She quietly walked to him, but she knew he felt her presence before she reached his side. He turned to her.

Elina placed her hands in his outstretched ones and felt the strong surety of his grip. The two stood staring at one another in silence. No words were shared, by neither mouth nor thought, but their eyes spoke volumes. Elina never dreamed such a change could come over her. Bravery and fear mingled inside her. She felt a confidence she had never before experienced, yet her fear of being separated from her husband by either of their deaths ran deep. She had only just found love. She couldn't lose it now.

Nilan continued to stare into his mate's eyes with thousands of feeling running through him, each one varying in degrees. How had he been blessed with this beautiful, valiant-spirited woman?

What had he done to deserve the privilege of standing by her side? What warranted this honor of defending her and helping her fight in this cause of truth and freedom?

Maybe this was the reason for his very existence, to be eternally bound to her and fight by her side. If it was, he grateful for the privilege. He pulled her close, and in his native tongue, whispered one of the many Inchant prayers against her ear.

"May our hands forever be strong,
our hearts forever be pure,
our cause forever be just,
our souls forever be true,
and our enemies forever fall before us."

Brutin stood before the group of men under his command. Their number covered the palace grounds and stretch beyond it. There was no speech, no counsel of war. The leader spoke three words in a voice that carried to every man's ears.

"To the death."

Twenty-eight

War

The Inchants touched down before the warriors could step a foot in the forest and the battle began immediately. Swords and arrows sliced through the air and cries of death came from both sides. Nilan and Elina fought side by side, each looking out for the other. Elina felt anger and sadness with each life she took, but she realized it could not be helped. They did not ask for this war. But it had come just the same. All they could do now was fight with all they had and end the evil.

Nilan pointed to a break through to the trees. He

and Elina raced to a tree, swiftly climbed up,

and unleashed a swarm of arrows, hitting every warrior they targeted. Their arms were like well -oiled machines, synchronized in their simultaneous assault. Sakriel and Gin sliced through the men, leaving numberless bodies in their wake. For each Inchant life lost, ten of Thenoch's men were taken.

Thenoch's soldiers were fierce, their voices crying victory with each Inchant they killed. While some of the men fought because they had no choice, others delighted in the bloodshed.

Elina wanted to cry each time an Inchant warrior fell but pushed her emotions deep inside and kept fighting. Her tunic was covered in the blood of her foes, but her lithe, strong body never stopped. At one point she heard a sudden growl behind her and turned to defend herself, but Nilan's arrow pierced the man's back before he could raise his blood-covered sword. She flashed her husband a brief look of gratitude before turning to fend off another warrior.

The battle raged on for what seemed like hours, but in fact was less than one. Soon, other than Sakriel and Gin, there were only weary Inchants left standing. Sakriel, Nilan, and his people took in the the sights and smell of war. Blood-covered bodies littered the land.

But the most important one was missing.

Sakriel turned toward the palace and the others followed. They must find Thenoch.

Twenty-nine

The Search

They searched the palace, taking down guards who tried to stop them along the way. They combed each and every room, but the dark lord was nowhere to be found.

Nilan ran a frustrated hand back through the hair that had loosened from his ponytail. "He must be here somewhere."

Gin stepped next to Nilan. "Knowing him, he most likely had a plan of escape."

Sakriel silently turned to Elina and met her knowing eyes with his own.

"He is here," she said. "I know where he is." She closed her eyes a moment. Of course she knew where he was. He was waiting for her–in the place that had once been her prison. He waited for her in all his arrogant glory. And she remembered exactly how to get there. The room would be forever engraved in her memory.

Nilan touched her arm and Elina opened her thoughts to his. His brow furrowed in anger, and after a brief moment, he nodded. He knew how this must end.

Elina turned back to Sakriel. "I am sure he is guarded by The Order."

"They will be taken care of," he said softly.

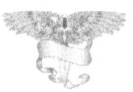

The men of The Order never knew what hit them. Nilan's arrows were the first to slice through the tower entrance, hitting three men instantly. The Inchants stormed the tower and the men never had a chance to defend themselves.

The way was cleared for Sakriel and Elina to

enter. They walked up the dark, narrow stairway.

A couple of bats squeaked as they flew over the passing heads ascending the tower steps. The walls were made of smooth round rocks. Touching them, Elina's mind flashed back to the night she escaped. She remembered the feel of the rocks as she kept her hand on the wall for guidance and ran down the stairs. The old man had laced the guards' bottle of Splendorfire with a sleeping ingredient
and they were both out cold by the time she reached the entrance. She could still remember both the
fear and the gratitude she felt that night.

When they reached the top of the tower, Sakriel paused to allow Elina a moment before opening the chamber door and stepping aside.

Thenoch was standing near the small window looking out over the city. He turned and smiled,
causing the open sores on his head to slowly ooze pus down over his dome-shaped scalp. His hideous smile widened when his eyes fell on Elina.

"My prize is back."

Elina shuddered inwardly, not from fear but revulsion. She had hoped she would never have to face the loathsome creature again. Her hope had been in vain. Facing Thenoch was her destiny. She quietly met Sakriel's eyes.

Yours is the purest and most valiant spirit in Dominae, therefore you are the only human strong enough for this. This quest is yours and yours alone. Your mate may be your support should
you need him, but you must end this.

When Elina nodded, he touched her cheek and left the room, and she turned back to Thenoch,
refusing to let her eyes roam around the dank cell. She kept her sight pinned on the creature that had
taken so many lives–the pitiful ruler who had taken away everyone she loved. Her mother, her brothers, even the old man who helped her escape, and last but certainly not least, her Inchant brothers and sisters. She did not have to know them all to love them, because she had become a part of them.

"You have lost." The strength in her voice rang against the stone walls.

"You think so?" He shook his head slightly and turned again to look out the window."

Elina was not swayed by his arrogance in the

slightest.

"Your facade has slowly diminished. Your true face has become clear. The evil that cankers your soul is now seen by the valiant few left in Dominae. Your reign is at an end. It is time for the cleansing of this kingdom."

Thenoch would have laughed, but looking down at the bodies strewn all over the courtyard, he knew the time of his amusement had passed. The streets ran red with the blood of Dominae citizens. There was no one left. All his supporters were dead, either killed in battle or killed trying to escape by The Order. Even Lucius, his spineless servant, was found hidden in the catacombs beneath the palace and immediately exterminated. The dark lord had no use for complete weaklings.

He finally turned back to Elina, his dark gaze taking in the changes in her. He would never have her now. He knew what he needed to do.

"No matter what you do," came his gargled voice, "I will always be powerful. After death, I will be even more so." He smiled. "We are always more powerful when we're dead. Did you not know this?"

Elina met his smile with a slight one of her own. "Without a body you cannot possibly be."

"Combined, we do not need a body, only a weak soul. Just one weak soul to begin with."

"That will never happen again."

"Oh, I assure you it will."

Those were the last words Thenoch spoke.

With lightening speed, Elina snatched a dagger from the scabbard hidden behind her back and watched it slice through the air and land in Thenoch's heart.

Elina opened the door and Nilan immediately took her in his arms. She drew back after a moment.

"It is not finished."

Gin looked around the two into the room at the fallen body. "What do you mean? Thenoch is dead."

"But it is not finished," Nilan said, repeating his wife's words.

Elina turned to Sakriel. "My lord, his body is dead, but his soul lingers. So do others."

"I know," Sakriel said. "Until their souls are bound, the land cannot renew itself."

"Then what do we do?" Gin asked, the furrow in his brow deepening.

Sakriel turned to Elina. "Think. The answer is inside you."

Elina was perplexed. "I know not what you mean. How could I know?"

"Think about all you heard while you were imprisoned here, both truths and myths."

It was hard, but Elina forced her mind to recall those days of being mistreated and malnourished, the days of bleakness and hopelessness. The only kindness shown to her at all was by the old man who helped her escape. When he brought her meals in, he would sometimes manage sneak in an extra piece of bread or over-ripened fruit. He would whisper things to her. Stories of things he had heard or things he'd witnessed. Sometimes he told her bits and pieces of long-forgotten fairy tales to bring a smile to her face. He shared little stories about the Inchant people. He had been a kind man.

Elina's minds raced over the things he told her,

but she couldn't remember any vital stories pertaining to Thenoch, other than the usual everyday deeds. Nothing the old man said really stood out in her mind. Except . . .

The man had made a comment about someone mentioning a myth about a hidden pool of dark souls. He said the person was immediately executed by The Order.

So why would Thenoch have a man executed for repeating a myth? Unless . . . it was not a myth.

Now she understood what Thenoch meant.

But . . . where would it be?

Then the answer came.

Nilan looked into Elina's eyes and searched her thoughts, his brows raising when he realized what she'd discovered. She finally spoke.

"We need to search the palace. We must find the Pool of Dark Souls."

When Sakriel nodded, Elina realized he had known all along.

Elina, Nilan, and the rest of the group search every nook and cranny of the palace but could not find the Pool of Dark Souls. They began searching outside the palace around the grounds. Still they found nothing. Elina fought back her frustration and began again. She couldn't stop. Everything inside her told her it was inside the palace. She had to find it. If she didn't, then all would be lost, for the evil would surely begin again. True, all the wicked were gone, but as long as the evil ones roamed free, the land would continue to die.

Standing in Thenoch's sleeping chamber once more, Elina turned desperate eyes to Sakriel.

"My lord, I know you know where it is. Will you not tell me?"

Sakriel's face expressed pain at her plea and it was evident that he wished he could tell her, but she must do this on her own. All he could do was guide her. He reached out and took her hand.

"The answer is inside you, Elina. Allow your mind to think of Thenoch. Think of his true character, see inside his mind and try to grasp his thinking."

Elina shuddered. The last thing she wanted to do

was imagine what Thenoch was thinking. The visions it might conjure up would be hideous.

"I know it is repulsive to think about," Sakriel said, guessing her thoughts, "but you must. Think on his true character, Elina. What drove him? What drives all those who choose evil over good?"

Elina began to let her thoughts drift to the dark lord. She had witnessed many facets of his character, all of them evil. She saw all the things that drove him—greed, selfishness, hatred, pride, arrogance, lust, jealousy, vanity. He seated himself above all others, placed himself on a pedestal, considered himself a god, possessing all power . . .

And where would a person with a god complex keep his power? As close to himself as possible.
He would not allow anyone else near the source of his power. Elina's eyes traveled the length of the room and noticed nothing was out of place.

Nothing except . . .

The large gold tapestry beneath the foot of the bed was crooked. Her eyes moved to Nilan's and before she could say a word, he quickly pulled up the tapestry and flung it across the room.

There at the foot of the bed was a small wooden door. Elina wondered why Thenoch hadn't covered it completely with the bed, then decided that he had probably become too weak to move it. And he wouldn't dare risk someone else finding out about the secrets he hid by commanding help.

Sakriel touched Elina's arm and she looked up at him.

"Now you must finish it. This is what you were chosen for."

Elina swallowed hard and nodded.

Nilan pulled open the door. Elina took a lamp from the dresser and lit it. She slowly headed down the stairs with Nilan close behind her.

J. Adams

Thirty

Vigilant In Valor

As soon as Elina descended the stairs, a strong breeze began to blow and she was glad she had brought a lantern instead of a candle. She was also glad Nilan was with her. No matter where they were, as long as he was beside her, she felt safe.

The closer they got to the bottom of the stairs, the stronger the wind became. They finally reached the bottom. Elina lifted the lamp and her eyes slowly adjusted. She scanned the cold room and reached for Nilan, suddenly feeling a little frightened.

"I am here, *sashana*," he said, wrapping his arms

around her.

She leaned back against his chest and they both stood in silence, taking everything in. They felt the evil surrounding them.

There were six grotesque stone heads protruding from the walls, each with a serpent hanging from its mouth between the teeth. Six winged lion-like statues stood around the room. Red velvet draped large stone tables placed in each corner, and each was topped with a bowl of red and black stones.

And at the center of the room, surrounded by eight meenabirds, stood the Pool of Dark Souls.

As if their presence were felt, the water began to bubble, spitting bloody acidic drops in the air, which immediately foamed, then turned to stone.

With Nilan's hand clasped tightly in hers, Elina walked toward the pool.

"Leave," a voice suddenly hissed, startling them both. "Leave."

Elina took a steading breath and heard herself say, "I will not."

The pool began to bubble even more, causing her to pause.

"Leave!" came the hiss again, only it was louder and had multiplied.

Feeling Nilan's steady hand in hers, she said again with more force, "I will not!" She watched the pool spit more drops into the air and turn to stone as they landed on the dirt.

A laugh rose from the pool followed by several others.

"Witness what shall happen to you if you come any closer!"

A large spray of the bloody water shot up from the middle and hit the ceiling, creating a stone stalagmite that hung over the pool.

Elina was afraid and Nilan could feel her fear with an intensity that made his heart pound. But it did not create fear in him. It created anger. He pulled her back gently and turned her to him. He tenderly touched her face.

"You were chosen for this task, *sashana*. And somehow I was found worthy enough to accompany you. I was deemed worthy of you. Your spirit is pure. Despite all you have gone through in your life, all you have lost, and all you have suffered, you have remained valiant. There is only goodness in you." He continued to caress her face. "You must do this. You are the only one who can. I will stay by your side. I will not leave you alone in this. I was not meant to. Have faith and all will be well. Faith and courage have brought you this far. Let them help you complete this task."

He pressed his forehead to hers and sent her all the strength he possessed. "Finish it, beloved," he whispered. "Finish it."

Elina did absorb his comfort and his strength. She stared into his eyes a moment before turning to face the bubbling pool. Swallowing her fear and pulling forth strength, faith, and courage she never knew she possessed, she approached the pool. The closer she got, the angrier the bloody liquid became. Yet the drops never touched either of them.

Suddenly several voices screeched in unison, "Leave!!!"

With Nilan gripping her waist, Elina stood at the side of the pool.

"I will not," she said a final time. "The time of evil has ended."

Calling on all her inner strength, she thrust her hand into the pool. In the next second, fire rose from the dark depths and circled her arm, yet she was not burned. Numberless voices began to wail loudly and the sound caused the ground to shake.

"She is killing ussss! Killing usssss! Killing usssss!"

The high-pitched voices reverberated through the chamber. The stone creatures beneath the tables, on the walls, and around the pool began to crumble, turning to dust before their eyes.

"Killing ussss! Killing ussss! Destroying ussss!" the voices continued to scream.

This went on and on for another long minute. Then, releasing a final wail, the pool disintegrated, taking the voices with it.

Other than Elina and Nilan's loud breathing, the chamber was silent. She finally turned to him. With tears streaming down their faces, they stared at one another for a long moment.

"It is finished," Elina whispered. "It is done."

Nilan nodded slightly, then suddenly crushed her against him and kissed her passionately, whispering over and over his love for her.

Elina soaked in his emotions and let them meld with her own. How she loved him! Even more so because he had been by her side through all of it. Even before she ever met him, he had been there for her, existed for her. Only neither of them had been aware of it.

She drew back and gazed into his eyes as her mind went over all the events of her life that led her to this point. All the hurt, the sorrow, and the pain. And all the joy.

Every single element had a purpose.

Each one had a place in the workings of what would be.

Each one had a place in the eternal way of things.

How grateful Elina was for her place in it!

Place in This World

Epilogue

Whole

Leaving the newly-beautified kingdom of Dominae had been harder for Elina than she thought it would be. She had watched the skies brighten, the snow melt, and the land turn green again. Even the desolate Vast Lands bloomed. Dominae merged with Anglann and Jubilus. New friendships were made and new trusts were forged. The evil of every kingdom was no more, having died away with the dark lords, and only the valiant remained.

Now, securely wrapped in Nilan's arms, Elina flew to her new home with her people, secure in the knowledge that her life would now endure for as long as that of the Inchants, that she and her husband truly would be bound until the end of time.

She was also secure in her knowledge that good really does triumph over evil–and a pure heart is worth more than all the treasures of the earth.

About the Author

J. (Jewel) Adams stays crazy busy with her family and writing. She has written several books in different genres and is also a motivational speaker to both youth and adult audiences. She home schools her four kids that are still at home, and between that and conjuring up new ideas for her books, her brain is completely fried most of the time. She and her husband Sean are the parents of eight children, which means they are both losing hair, but hey, that's what Rogaine is for, right?

In her spare time (when she has any) she likes to curl up with a good book and a healthy stash of orange Tic Tacs. She and her family reside in Utah.

Jewel loves hearing from her fans, so if you would like to contact her to tell her how much you love her books or give her sympathy for the fried brain, or suggestions for the hair loss problem (for her husband, of course) contact her at **jewela40@gmail.com**

Also visit her website and blog at **jadamsnovels.com** and **jewelsbestgems.blogspot.com**

Books by J. Adams/Jewel Adams

The Journey – YA Fantasy

Against the Odds – Contemporary Romance

Mercedes' Mountain – Contemporary Romance

E-books

The Wishing Hour – Romantic Sci-Fi Fantasy

Of Blessings and Dreams: The Legacy – LDS Contemporary Romance

Tears of Heaven – LDS Contemporary Romance

Place In This World: The Sequel to The Journey – YA Fantasy

The Journey – YA Fantasy

For Love of Angel – YA Romance

Elise's Heart – YA Romance

Children's E-book

Forbidden Portals: The Quicksilver Project